PUSHKIN PRESS

HIDEO FURUKAWA, born in 1966, is an acclaimed and prize-winning writer, hailed by many in Japan's literary world as a prodigy worthy of inheriting the mantle of Haruki Murakami. He was awarded the Mishima Prize in 2006 for *Love*. His best-known novel is the 2008 *Holy Family*, an epic work of alternate history set in north-eastern Japan, where he was born.

DAVID BOYD has translated stories by Toh EnJoe, Genichiro Takahashi and Hiroko Oyamada, among others. He holds a Master's degree from the University of Tokyo and is currently a PhD candidate at Princeton University. He lives in Los Angeles, California.

D0581515

HIDEO FURUKAWA

SLOW BOAT

A SLOW BOAT
TO CHINA RMX

translated by
DAVID BOYD

PUSHKIN PRESS

SERIES EDITORS: David Karashima and Michael Emmerich
TRANSLATION EDITOR: Elmer Luke

Pushkin Press
71–75 Shelton Street
London, WC2H 9JQ

2002-nen no surō bōto by FURUKAWA Hideo
Copyright © 2006 by FURUKAWA Hideo

Chugoku-yuki no surō bōto RMX by FURUKAWA Hideo
Copyright © 2003 by FURUKAWA Hideo

English Translation copyright © 2017 by David Boyd

English translation rights arranged with FURUKAWA Hideo
through Japan UNI Agency, Inc. Tokyo

First published by Pushkin Press in 2017

The publisher gratefully acknowledges the support of the
British Centre for Literary Translation and the Nippon Foundation

1 3 5 7 9 8 6 4 2

ISBN 978 1 782273 28 8

Designed and typeset in Marbach by Tetragon, London
Printed by CPI Group (UK) Ltd, Croydon, CR0 4YY

www.pushkinpress.com

CONTENTS

BOAT ONE
THE DIG

I've never made it out of Tokyo.

I can't tell you how many times I've asked myself if the boundary is real. Of course it's real. And if you think I'm lying, you can come and see for yourself.

I'm working on the final plan today. For the last time.

The boundary isn't a border. But just because you don't need a passport doesn't mean you can up and leave whenever you like. This is where I was born, and it's where I'm going to die.

This is my botched Tokyo Exodus, the chronicle of my failures.

Three failures, to be exact. The Japanese language is nothing but lies. Or maybe just chaos. "What happens twice will happen again." OK, I buy that. But how can that idea coexist with "Third time's the charm"?

Farewell, mother tongue.

Still, I'm writing this in Japanese. It's the best language I have for writing down my experiences (or the contents of my brain). No question. Language has its limits, but it's all we've got. For understanding each other or misunderstanding each other or whatever. Besides, isn't life all about limits?

At the end of the day, we've all got our limits. As living things, we're bound to die.

Death.

Let me tell you about the Big Limit.

Tokyo, 2002 A.D.

Winter. K-1 kick-boxer Ernesto Hoost shouts: "I'm the three-time champion!" Good for you. I've failed to make it out of Tokyo three times. The first time, I guess I was ten or eleven. Not sure which. How old are you in the fifth grade? That old. My most recent fail was a little under two years ago.

Three tries, three girlfriends.

The losses don't stop. The odds were always stacked against me. Sneaking onto some ship is probably my best hope to get out now.

Maybe you figured this out already—I don't do well with people. Believe me, I tried. But we need to keep on fighting, right? Even if we're just marching towards death.

No—that's exactly why we need to stay in the ring.

It's morning, 24th December. I'm at Hamarikyu Gardens, making a fist.

This is the last time. My final plan, ergo my ultimate plan. So I need to get a good read on things. I tell myself: dig, dig, dig. *Think archaeologically.*

Hamarikyu is between the Tsukiji Fish Market, Takeshiba Pier and Shiodome (where the Shiosite skyscrapers are going up as we speak). I'm looking at the moment that Tokyo Bay becomes the Sumida River. Wait. More like I'm watching the Sumida lose its name.

Time—so much time—flows by in a liquid state.

Thick, leaden liquid.

The water buses aren't running.

Of course they aren't. It's 9.20 in the morning. First day after a long weekend. Christmas festivities will bring crowds later on, but there's nobody here now. Just me and the dark clouds. Wait, was it supposed to rain today? Did I miss the forecast? The whole place is empty, but this bus terminal feels like a mortuary.

Thick, leaden sky.

I open the pamphlet I got at the ticket gate. Hamarikyu once belonged to the Tokugawa family. Property of the Shogunate. After the Meiji Restoration, it was an imperial villa. During the American Occupation, it lost its imperial standing. Just makes you wonder... who really owns Tokyo? I walk around. There are a couple of spots for duck-hunting, used even in the middle of the Pacific War. There's a peony garden—not that peonies are in season. There's Shiori Pond, the only saltwater pond in Tokyo. I see a lot of birds. Taking another look at the pamphlet, I can see that this place gets all sorts of avian visitors. Resident birds: wagtail, spot-billed duck, night heron, little grebe... Then the migratory birds: common pochard, northern shoveler, northern pintail, etc. But the bird you see the most makes no appearance in the garden's official literature: the crow.

The jungle crow, to be specific. A very intelligent (and impudent) scavenger.

At this hour, the garden belongs to the crows. They fly around, hang upside-down from the pines, hop across the grass. There's a party of crows by Shiori Pond, cawing and cawing. They're making a racket, so I walk over to see what all the fuss is about.

They're going at a carcass. Maybe it was a seagull.

And I was under the impression that eating in the garden was strictly prohibited.

Not that you'd know it from the pamphlet, but the crows make their nests high up in the trees. They swoop down and attack lesser birds. They take total advantage of all the nature Hamarikyu has to offer. They do what they want.

I feel a kind of love for this place, where crows can be crows.

But that fantasy doesn't last long.

I hear something like screams. I follow my ears, off the path—off-limits. I walk up a low grassy hill, and there it is. A huge enclosure, boarded up to look like something legit. Clearly, they don't want anyone to know what's going on.

I peek between the cracks. About ten crows inside, alive, but very unhappy. What the hell is this?

There's a sign on the boards: WILD CROW REGULATION INSTALLATION—PROPERTY OF METROPOLITAN TOKYO.

Meaning: Hands off.

For the peace of the citizens of Tokyo.

The captive crows thrash around. They're frantic.

The screaming doesn't stop:

Let us outta here! Let us outta here!

But this is necessary, to make Tokyo a better place for us to live.

Crows have no value to people, so we exterminate them.

Hands off.

If you can't comply, then Tokyo has no need for you, either.

In that instant, I slip into a daydream. A fury. I fantasize about prying off the boards and busting the bars, freeing the crows. I want to find the other cages (this can't be the only one) and destroy them, too. But my legs don't move. And I know why. I'm not afraid of being caught by some cop or security guard with a nightstick. Like I could care. Here's my problem: If a cop comes after me, do I have what it takes to fight back? Like, call him a STUPID DICKHEAD and lunge right at him? I don't think so. And there's only one reason for that. I'm not naïve enough to think I can free the crows. Not really. If someone like me breaks into the cage and lets the birds out, they'll just step up security. They'll have ten new crows in there, like, right away. And they'll keep a closer watch on them. The incident would end up on the news, too, giving the citizens of Tokyo more reason to hate crows. And the cop trying to stop me, he doesn't give a shit about the crows. He's just doing his job. He doesn't care about me or anything I have to say. Justice isn't in the picture.

If the law forbids it, you can't do it. That's it. End of story.

The Holocaust was OK under Nazi German law.

That's why my legs won't move. Why I feel empty. Alone.

Dark clouds.

Christmas Eve in Hamarikyu, and no one is around.

Where's the rain?

I wasn't so weak when I was young. But I got old. Now I always think about consequences. Through my early twenties, when I was sure justice was on my side, justice was on my side.

Now I can barely utter the word "justice".

There were times when I stood up and fought back. And I lost. Three times.

Days of failed escapes. When I was younger, and tougher. When I was sure there was a way out.

BOAT TWO
KEEP BOTH HANDS
FLAT ON YOUR LAP

I stopped going to school when I was in the fifth grade—in early May, right after Golden Week. Everyone always wants to know why. I had my reasons, trust me. My mom was getting hysterical, for starters. And my teacher was always coming to my house and getting me in trouble... Talk about no boundaries. But I bet *they* saw things differently. I bet, the way they saw it, it wasn't me who was giving up on school. School was giving up on me.

Whatever, not even close.

I know what happened. But it's hard for me to explain, even now. Way harder for a kid ten or eleven years old to put into words—into *Japanese*.

Anyway... I guess what really triggered it was Children's Day. "When you write 'Children's Day', don't do it in *kanji*," my teacher said. "Spell it out in *kana*. If you can read the *kanji* for 'children' then you're not a child any more." *Ha ha ha*. Hilarious.

The whole world was comfortably dumb.

Children's Day: *A day for the children, for their happiness and for their mothers.*

Give me a break. As soon as I saw all the carp floating over the city, that was it for me. What the hell is this farce?

Tokyo's full of carp (or streamers acting like carp). What are all these fish-mouths trying to say? It's a giant farce. True, "farce" wasn't in my vocabulary back then. But that's what I felt, in my bones. I had to get the hell out.

Which is what I did, in dreams.

Not ambitions. Real dreams, if dreams can be real.

I said it before and I'll say it again. This record of mine is nothing without my Japanese and all of its limits. When you talk about life, you have to talk about the Big Limit. Death. It's a part of life. No escaping it.

OK. Let's start at the beginning.

Pretty sure it was the end of the fourth grade. February probably. February 1985. I went to sleep. Except I didn't. After a few minutes in bed, not sleeping, I had this revelation. It just came to me. I might've been a stupid kid, but this fact hadn't hit me until that night. Suddenly I understood: *I'm going to die at some point. My life won't last forever.*

I curl up.

That night, alone in bed, I started seeing time differently. History. Followed by a full stop. Try to imagine what it's like for a fourth-grader to be terrified of death. I had to find a way out. Sleep was definitely scary—a whole lot like death. But that didn't keep me from getting sucked in.

Into the world of dreams.

The boy who is afraid of death lives for dreams.

I started my dream diary before entering the fifth grade. But writing down your dreams isn't as easy as you think, so I went looking for help. A guide. Something to point the way. What I found was a how-to book. Dream analysis stuff. Like Freud (yeah, Sigmund Freud). "Snakes represent penises, caves represent vaginas." That sort of thing. But the real Freud is too complicated for a total beginner. Hell, I still haven't read *Introduction to Psychoanalysis*. The book I bought wasn't the real Freud. It was *Freudian*. Written by a so-called "expert", published by a so-called "publisher". But this book became my bible. It was easy to read. The chapters were short, and there were tons of illustrations. It almost felt like a strategy guide for some video game. Cheat codes for the libido or something.

But what's a vagina to a prepubescent boy anyway?

Sure. I'd had some sex dreams. But I never saw the female anatomy as the be-all and end-all. Well, I never saw the female anatomy at all. In my dreams, there was nothing but skin down there. Smooth, like a doll's. You can't dream about something you've never seen in the real world. I hadn't come yet, either, so all the references to "ejaculation" meant jack to me.

Reading dreams is hard.

I tried my best. I was a big fan of free association. The moment I woke up, I would write down how my dreams *felt*, using a few clues picked up from my bible. You have to start somewhere. Can't write about your dreams without the language of dreams.

The problem wasn't *me*—not necessarily. The Japanese language has its own shortcomings. But that's a story for another time.

This is the story of a fifth-grade boy hell-bent on making

sense of his dreams. Cracking the code. And that means staring death in the face. Which takes, you know, courage. In the words of Henry Miller, "Sleep is an even greater danger than insomnia." Or did he mean something else? Maybe I've got it wrong.

Story of my life.

Back in the world of the living: Children's Day. 5th May 1985. Flying fish invade Tokyo airspace. But I'm not there. I'm in bed.

I was so devoted to figuring out my dreams that I never left my bed. I kept on sleeping. Didn't go to school.

That's how I became a "dropout".

What happened then?

By the end of June, I was no longer a resident of Suginami ward. The guidance counsellor at school recommended "a change of environment". For me. Not my family. They stayed put. I was sent away, on my own, to an alternative school for dropouts. A place for kids who are for some reason unable to go to regular school. There were grade-schoolers—like me—and middle-schoolers. We lived together under one roof, in a dorm. And, following our marching orders, we walked to and from the local school each day. Together.

Out there in the mountains. It kind of felt like summer camp.

But we were still in Tokyo.

Japan Railways, JR, by that name, didn't exist yet. It was National Railways. Well after the NR Chuo Line stops to the west, Tokyo keeps on going. I never thought about it until then. After Takao? Another prefecture, right? Saitama or Yamanashi or something. Beyond my ken. Hell, I was oblivious to the fact that Tokyo has eight "villages". Did *you* know that? Tokyo's eastern limit: Minamitori Island. Formerly known as Marcus Island. Part of the Ogasawara Islands. Co-ordinates: 153° 58' 50" E. To the south: the Okinotori Islands. An atoll, actually, almost completely underwater at high tide. 20° 25' N. Uninhabited, obviously, and far and away Tokyo's southernmost point.

Tokyo.

How far does Tokyo go?

There I was. A ten- or eleven-year-old dropout with no interest in speaking to others. Sent away—to the only Tokyo "village" on the main island. Damn close to Tokyo's western edge.

I was shocked to find Tokyo went that far. It took me two trains (the Chuo and Ome Lines) and one bus (called the West Tokyo Line for a reason) to get there. A solid two hours from home—and I'm still in Tokyo? Are you kidding? For one thing, this place is *deep* in the mountains. For another, the news-stand at the station is selling wasabi... *The news-stand.*

It felt like Chichibu Tama National Park.

Nothing around, unless you're itching for a killer hike. And the dorm was apparently built on land that used to be a village for fugitive warriors.

"Fugitive warriors"?

*

The village school had opened its doors to us dropouts. Due to a dwindling student body, it had to shut down or agree to educate a wild bunch of losers from all over Japan. It chose door number two and stayed open. That was what everyone wanted—the teachers, the village, everyone. And in my own (unasked-for) opinion, it was the right move. Right?

That's how I see it at present.

Now, technically, the dorm was for grade-schoolers. But, like I said before, there were some older kids, too. When a dropout was unable to drop back into life, they were allowed to stick around. Indefinitely.

I have more to tell you about the dorm, but let me say something about the school first. It's a little embarrassing— I can't remember the name of the place. Wonder why. No, I'm pretty sure I know why. Some kind of complex, some deep desire...

When I first got there, the school felt like it was at the end of the world. So, for lack of a better option, I'm going to call it "The End of the World Elementary".

OK. Back to the dorm.

Shit hit the fan as soon as I arrived. I wasn't allowed to keep sleeping in. DORM is a four-letter word. Right up there with FUCK or SHIT. It really was the "change of environment" they said I needed. No joke. My world was violently upended. The director was of the professional opinion that my attachment to my bed represented "a deep desire to return to the womb". Or something like that. So when it was time to get up in the morning, she had my bed taken away. Rise and shine.

"Get up! Time to go to school!"

So I got up. I went to school.

And that was the end of my dream diary. I mean, there were other factors for this. Maybe you figured this out already—the director was a practising psychoanalyst, an expert in all things Freud, probably in her late thirties. When I got to the dorm, the analyst in me had little choice but to scram. I might have been a really ignorant kid, but even I knew that Freud was a total relic. Session's up, Herr Freud. Plus, I wasn't allowed to bring my bible to the dorm (they were pretty strict about what you could have there), and the place had zero privacy. What if someone got their hands on my dreams? Just thinking about it sent shivers down my spine. It'd be like someone messing with your corpse.

And something told me that the director wouldn't hesitate to sneak a peek.

She was a shrink, after all.

So that put a stopper in my dream-diving. This sucks. I cursed the so-called reality they forced me back into.

That also marked my return to education. Every morning, I made the trek to school with everyone else. To The End of the World.

They made me.

OK. About the other kids. What kind of "pupils" were they? What did these dropouts have in common? Not a damn thing. Each one was like a snowflake. Like, unique. Well, some were sort of typical. They got chronic headaches or stomach aches. Some simply couldn't stomach school lunches. There were perfectionists and the opposites of perfectionists. Fat kids and skinny kids, bullies and cry-babies. It was a zoo—a human zoo.

One kid per cage.

We were like brothers. And sisters. There were girls in the dorm, too. Our living quarters were strictly separated, but we made the walk to school and back together.

There's one more thing I need to mention about The End of the World.

It wasn't bad. When I first saw the village, I was convinced I was going to be stuck in some shabby, cobweb-infested schoolhouse. All wood, no windows—just a giant box. But that was all in my head. This place was all right, not in any way inferior to my school in Suginami.

Really, if I had to choose, I'd say I was happier at The End of the World.

The ruins of the stone Buddha (nothing left but his ankles) on the way to school. The thatched roofs on old farmhouses we could see from the schoolyard. The smell of dirt and grass all around us. Now and then, misguided cicadas would land on the monkey bars and cry their hearts out. Even in class, we could hear thirty different kinds of birds singing outside. Behind the school a warning sign read: BEWARE OF BEARS. This place had it all.

But—most important of all—*she* was there.

She showed up about three weeks after I did.

The day after the last day of school, a new load of loser-track kids gets dropped off. Seven boys, four girls. Summertime at Camp Dropout. Even though I'm still pretty new to the place, I find myself playing mentor to kids even newer to this game than me.

We line up, face-to-face, checking each other out. Nobody says a thing. Not a hello, nothing.

And there she is. She's in the sixth grade—a year above me—and I guess you could say she's a looker. Except my eyes aren't on her face. Because the magnetic thing about her is, like, her... chest. I mean, *whoa*. My first impression: this girl has some serious boobs.

I'm a little young to notice things like that, but I've got stirrings. And something kicks in, makes me stare. This girl's not a freak or anything, but stuffed into her tight little bra are the finest, fullest-formed sixth-grade boobs in the Greater Tokyo Metropolitan Area. Some things you just can't hide. And some things are hard to ignore. (I guess I wasn't ideal mentor material.)

Aside from her boobs, nothing about this girl really stood out. At first meeting, that is. But within twenty-four hours, it's clear to everyone that she's nothing like the rest of us. What's so different about her? Not what you're thinking. It's her *mouth*. It never shuts. Ever.

This girl talks and talks and talks.

Talk—even a lot of talk—isn't necessarily rare or weird, either. But in my brief time on this planet, I'd never met anyone who talked *the way she talked*. I was amazed. To use the language I have now, I'd call it hyper-talk—not over-talk. She doesn't blab endlessly on some boring subject, or gossip about stupid things, or ask a bunch of mind-numbing questions. Blabber like that I could handle. All the kids could. Because that's how kids are. But she was on a different plane. If she was just darting around, hitting sixty topics in under a minute, we could've coped. No sweat. But what came pouring out of her mouth was more like a mash of sixty conversations happening simultaneously—*jump jump jump*—and she'd go on like that for an hour straight, barely stopping to breathe. What do you do with that? No way you could, like, try to have a conversation with her. What's she saying? Total gibberish, right? Maybe. Maybe not.

She was like an alien.

Or maybe she was manic? No, this was something else, something—I don't know—superhuman? I was only ten or eleven at the time, same as the others. But I felt something, like an aura. I could tell she wasn't fake. She was kind of real. Like, her hyper-talk was about something deep. Even someone in their twenties probably wouldn't get it—forget about a bunch of grade-school rejects. No hope. So the kids kept their distance.

Within a couple of days, her mouth had totally devastated our peace and quiet (if we ever had such a thing). She rattled everyone's cage.

In class, it was even worse. We were supposed to be on summer break, but class went on at The End of the World. Like always, only different. For the summer, misfits of all grades were thrown into a single classroom. The powers that be had some plan in mind, to get us to adjust, or readjust, to being in a school environment, being around other students. It was a strange sort of rehab. They wanted us to communicate with other students and relate to kids in other grades.

Communicate.

Her hyper-talk ruined any chance of that happening.

We didn't have assigned seats. It was, like, sit anywhere, next to your friends, or some kid you don't know, or on your own—if that's your thing.

The director was like a saint, kind and easy. But the kids were not.

"Back off, weirdo."

"Ugh. Don't even think about sitting here—I don't care what grade you are."

"Omigod. Shutupshutupshutupshutup. Put a sock in it!"

"Pleeeze, does anyone have a spare pair of headphones? I can't take it any more."

"Yo, Grade Six," somebody yells to her, "try speaking Japanese for once!"

"I *am* speaking Japanese!" she yells back. Then—two seconds later—she's back in orbit, rambling about some alien life form. Next thing you know, she's going:

"... Millions-in-Ethiopia-starved-to-death..."

Then, without skipping a beat:

"... You-ever-see-*Eight-Samurai*-with-Hiroko-Yakushimaru?"

You who? Anybody, I guess.

Anybody at all. But who could respond to that? By the time she says something, she's already in the middle of the next thing.

Our class was totally at the mercy of her careening motor-mouth.

And where was I in all this?

Sitting there, speechless. I didn't talk for the longest time. The other kids left me alone, or left me out... of everything. Now, for the first time, I was watching it happen to another kid. They avoided her like the plague, rejected her, shut her out.

I didn't share their view of her. For me, it was the total opposite. I wanted to get closer. I mean, yeah, I wanted a closer look at her boobs, too, but that wasn't all...

Activities, activities. Before summer started, they had us play sports or "pitch in" with garden work. Around ten days after I got there, they had a big party for the Star Festival. One Sunday, we all went into the mountains, to pick wild plants or something.

But summer was different. Every day was something. Going to Okutama to check out the giant trees, making charcoal, making noodles from scratch, even going to the local hot spring. *A healthy body is a happy body.* They kept us moving. Volunteers, counsellors and occasional social workers. This was our so-called summer break, and we were busier than ever.

OK, flash to the main event: the big barbecue.

We take a bus to the Akigawa River. We're given tasks. Mine is setting up the grill, which I manage to make level, despite my serious clumsiness. When we finish our jobs, we can do anything we want until it's time to cook and eat. *Free time.* Some kids hang around the director, asking barbecue-related questions or whatever. Some other kids—they called themselves "explorers"—get lessons from a local guy on making goggles from bamboo segments to check out the river bottom. Some other kids—outsiders with nowhere to go—head down to the river to skip stones.

When it's time to start cooking, I get closer to the girl—through a three-step process. Step one: hop. We're skewering kebabs at the director's instruction. Onion, corn, eggplant, beef. Fresh fish from the river. The girl's sitting there, gleefully piercing a marshmallow.

"... and-the-Marshmallow-Man-bounced-through-the-city..."

"I ain't afraid of no ghost," I say, almost in reflex, as I wrestle with a gnarly red bell pepper. She stops and turns and looks right at me—big smile on her face.

"*Ghostbusters*, right?" I say, pleased with myself. "I saw it over New Year's. Wasn't sure if it was supposed to be funny or scary." It's been seven months, so my memory of the movie is a little sketchy. Still, I'm pretty sure she was talking about the final scene.

She opens her mouth to respond. But what comes out doesn't really sound like a response. It has nothing to do with ghosts or marshmallows or anything. More like she's weighing the pros and cons of dance parties. And the words just keep coming.

Coming at me.

Wha—? Dance parties?

Total gibberish, like I said.

I just smile. Don't know what else to do.

She's smiling, too—saying something about, like, a mermaid with human legs.

Mermaid? Because this is a river? Wait, don't mermaids live in the ocean? A mermaid could never survive in the Akigawa. The water's way too shallow... you'd need a freshwater imp, like a *kappa*... shit, now *I'm* jumping around. Anyway, before I know it, the mermaid's history.

But we had a real moment there. A close encounter of the third kind.

Step two: skip. When we finish eating, we're supposed to make art with stones we found in the river. We're supposed to think about the shape of the rock or how it feels in our hands and, with that in mind, draw something on it. Presto—a rock of art.

This was almost twenty years ago. I have no memory of what my rock looked like. But I definitely remember hers. Her mouth moving at warp speed—like always —and there was this force field all around her. So no one got close. That's why I had no problem seeing what she was making, even though she was pretty far away. At first, I thought she was drawing a drowned body. Or maybe a dog? But the neck was too long for that. It had a dog's face, but the body started to look like... a dragon.

I know that dragon! I've seen it somewhere.

No, I didn't "see" it. I *saw* it—at the movies.

Time out. What if everything she says comes from movies? What if everything she knows comes from movies?

What if she's not just making them up?

Maybe she's bouncing from one world to the next—World A, World B, C, D, E, F... all the way to Z, and beyond. Maybe I'm beginning to understand. Like, make Japanese out of what she's saying. Not everything, but most of it, maybe.

So this dragon-like creature—it's got to be Fal-something, the Luck Dragon. From *The NeverEnding Story*. I saw it over spring break. On a movie screen. Which was what we did in 1985. Remember? Before VHS was the one format to rule them all. Back when Beta was still around. When, if you wanted to rent something, you had to pick which way to go. 1985. Movies hadn't really come home yet.

You had to *go* to the movies—the movie theatre.

I didn't really know movies—only went three or four times a year. I was more into dreams... Then it hit me, like a bolt of lightning. Her movies are just like my dreams! All I have to do is imagine that everything coming out of her mouth is a dream. *Analyse.* Sure, I'm only ten or eleven, but I've had a bit of training. Shit, I was well on my way to cracking the dream code. Before they took all my dreams away.

But now I have a new one. *Her.*

Step three: jump. Read her like a dream.

On the bus ride home, I listen carefully to every syllable that speeds out of her mouth. I map all of her jumps, from dimension to dimension. I don't let the sudden changes of scene throw me. I don't worry about plots or anything. I just try to get a *feel* for the worlds she's visiting. Just like when I was writing down my dreams. I concentrate on the sense of her words. This might work after all. Long live Freud!

Movies. That was the key.

She's not rehashing stories. She's reliving the scenes.

A scene comes to life in her head. Then she moves on to another.

It's like she's playing twenty to thirty heroines at once. Or maybe she casts herself in minor roles. Maybe she's only a spectator. As I watch her leap from one world to the next, I take a step into hers.

The problem is that she's seen every movie ever made. I've never seen *Splash* or *Poltergeist* or *Footloose* or *Dune*. But it all works out. As long as I know that she's playing the parts of all these different people—or aliens or dancers or mermaids—each with a different story. I just need to keep a couple of basic rules in mind. First: *Her world is actually twenty or thirty different worlds. Like a solar system.* Second: *No matter how things look or sound, she's still in there, somewhere.*

Is that a yodel?

Sounds like a nightmare, right?

But I can follow.

By the time the bus pulls up to the dorm, I have a mental log of her several alien worlds.

In class, there's an empty seat next to her. Of course there is. Because no one's deranged enough to sit there. Except, well, me.

I sit down next to her (and her boobs) and say, "Hey".

*

For the first couple of hours, she's still jabbering away, but with a look of total shock on her face. Like she can't believe she's actually communicating. It takes some time for it to click—someone else is wading through the muck of her mixed-up movie worlds with her.

Her words are getting through.

This is where strangers meet.

An alien makes contact with one of her own.

For the first time, maybe ever, she realizes that she *wants* to communicate. Then, just like that, she's talking to me, at hyper-speed.

So I start decoding her, my dream girl, at hyper-speed.

I spent the rest of my summer learning all sorts of things about her. Like why she knew—and how she could remember—all those movies.

"I saw them over and over."

"Over and over?"

"I was at the movies, all day."

"What do you mean—why?"

"When Mommy doesn't want me around, she gives me a movie ticket (she has an endless roll of them—I think they're a shareholder perk or something), and orders me to stay there."

She tells me all about her little sister—her half-sister—who stays at home when my dream girl is sent (alone) to the movies. Kind of sounds like my dream girl is being *banished*. She sees the same movie over and over. She sits in the back row, by the door. That way, when Mommy calls, the staff at the movie theatre know where to find her. They relay Mommy's orders: *You can come home now.*

(Pretty sure I don't have to remind you that nobody had cell phones in 1985. Phone cards had only been around for a couple of years.)

On standby until Mommy calls. She has things to eat and drink, and she goes to the toilet whenever she needs to. Otherwise, she sits back and enjoys the shows. She sucks them in—or they suck her in. She remembers everything.

She's seen *Once Upon a Time in America*—a brutally long film about a brutal Jewish mobster. Too complicated for any kid to wrap her head around. Still, she's dipped into that world.

She's seen *Gremlins*. Three rules for Mogwai owners to live by.

She's seen *The Terminator*. An unkillable assassin sent back from the future.

She talks and talks. She shares her worlds with me. Worlds I've never known.

It's almost like communing with the spirit world.

I read her at hyper-speed. And I fall for her at hyper-speed. She keeps me well fed with fresh dreams. And because I'm probably the first person in her life to kind of understand her, she wants to be close to me, too. This isn't *like*—this is *love*.

Our dates are limited to The End of the World and its remote territories. That basically means the bus stop, the local shrine, the village office, the hot springs, the mountain trail. Our forest friends surround us: the graceful mourning cloak, the ultra-ultramarine flycatcher, the serow that the other kids see as a three-headed hellhound. Of course, all we do on our dates is talk. Just talk. Or—the way I saw it—interpret dreams.

Our dreams go everywhere we go. We have access to twenty or thirty different worlds (how many are there, really?), far beyond the reach of—and of no interest to—the others. But we never badmouth them. We never look down on them.

All that matters to me is that she's happy with how we are. *We*. Me and my sixth-grade girlfriend.

My first girlfriend.

My most momentous moment at The End of the World happened in the schoolyard—by "the weather station", the closest thing we had to a monument. And it was monumental. When my first girlfriend gave me my first kiss. History of mine! Let the day be marked.

She's two or three centimetres taller than me, so she sort of ducks down to kiss me. Her boobs hit me in the chest—with a good amount of force, too. This is all really new to me, but I'm surprised they don't feel softer. What a letdown. I blame it on the bra.

In the moment, I have no idea what our kiss means.

I have no idea what it means when—for the first time ever—she stops talking.

"Everybody get on the bus," the director is shouting. "Find a seat, and keep both hands flat on your lap."

My memory gets a little fuzzy after that kiss. All data for the next twelve hours or so is irretrievable—forever lost. But the next big scene I remember, for sure. It was Lake Okutama. Maybe we were visiting Ogochi Dam? Or the Centre for Water and Nature?

It was the last day of summer break.

Could have been 31st August, or not. Does it really matter? All I know is that it was the day my beautiful summer came to a cold, brutal end.

The bus was idling in the parking lot. I was following the director's orders—lining up to get back on the bus. But, after a couple of seconds, I realized something.

She isn't here.

It smacks me like a whip. Red alert. Alarm bells are ringing. WHERE. IS. SHE? I do a three-sixty—to get a full scan of the parking lot. I see her. There. Over by that stupid red sports car. There's a woman in her thirties standing by the passenger door, a man in sunglasses—age unclear—in the driver's seat. The woman's talking to somebody.

To *her*. My girlfriend.

I watch my girlfriend squeeze into the back seat of the car.

But she's looking back. Looking at the bus. Looking for me. Our eyes meet and sparks fly. The alarm in my brain goes off. *BEEP BEEP BEEP BEEP.*

That woman has to be Mommy, here to take my girlfriend home.

How could I be so dumb?

I never saw this coming. I never thought she was going to be taken away. When she showed up at the start of summer, I was convinced she was here for the long haul, like the rest of us. But she was just a summer camper. Sent to The End of the World to stay out of Mommy's hair, until Mommy came back.

She was being taken away.

We were going separate ways. That was our fate.

But I had been too stupid to notice.

Red alert.

Once my girlfriend was buckled up in the back seat, the car took off. I broke out of line and ran after it. What was the director saying? *Keep both hands flat on your lap?* Are you kidding me? More like, *keep both hands on your girlfriend and never let go.*

Never let go.

I leap onto the highway that runs next to the lake. The highway that runs here all the way from Hikawa Campsite. National Route 411. I'm a hitchhiker with an emergency. The station wagon coming towards me screeches to a stop. Well, more like I bring it to a stop by standing in the way. They were probably yelling at me, but I don't remember. I think they were campers, in their twenties.

I'm all worked up. "They took my sister!" I scream. "Follow that red car!"

It all sounded very dramatic—and they took my word for it.

I mean, it was a lie they could believe. My girlfriend was banging on the rear window, crying and screaming, playing her part to perfection. Saying *something*—to me.

"Come on! Catch them!" I yell. The station-wagon driver floors it. The adults in that sports car had to be completely unprepared for the station wagon speeding after them—this was a scene from a movie they hadn't seen. We chase them through tunnel after tunnel—Omugishiro, Murosawa, Sakamoto. Drumcan Bridge to our left. Flying west down NR 411.

We're getting close to Kamosawa. As in: "Kamosawa, Yamanashi Prefecture".

Tokyo's about to end.

And we're catching up. I scream: "Ram them! Make them stop!"

But next thing I know, we get cut off. Something pulls between the station-wagon (that I kinda sorta hijacked) and the sports car. It's the bus, sliding sideways, blocking the whole highway. The station wagon swerves to a stop.

The bus driver sped up and killed the chase.

A highway with only two lanes. Game over—just like that.

There's a sign up ahead: "Now entering Yamanashi Prefecture". End of Tokyo.

I fling open the station-wagon door and bound onto the street. I try to run past the bus. But arms grab me, hold me back. Adult arms. I struggle, start swinging like a maniac—I know justice is on my side. Give her back! You can't have her!

But Kamosawa, Yamanashi is off-limits.

No matter what.

No way out of Tokyo.

That was how I lost my first girlfriend.

BOAT THREE

I CAN READ SOME, NOT OTHERS

I toss a pebble into the well of my consciousness.

A rock of art? Does it have a dragon's face on it?

Back to 24th December 2002.

I had to move on. I couldn't take it. It was killing me to see the Hamarikyu crows locked up that way. Change of plans. I got on the New Transit Yurikamome Line at Shiodome Station. A train that would take me as far as the city goes in that direction. Odaiba. But I wasn't going for the night scene—it was morning and Odaiba was dead. I looked around for signs of life. The Palette Town Ferris wheel was up and running from 10 a.m. As always, Fuji TV's globe-shaped observatory was hanging in mid-air—looking over everything like a transparent eyeball.

Minato ward and Shinagawa ward converge by the Grand Meridien Hotel. Tokyo's front line. I get off at Odaiba Station, walk across West Park Bridge and enter Symbol Promenade Park. The heart of Odaiba. A hollow surrounded by semi-futuristic buildings.

No rain. Not yet. Is it coming or not?

I find a seat and let the morning chill seep in. Through my coat and my jeans.

Does this even pass for a seat? More like a stone frustum. A man-made stalagmite with the head cut off. There's more than one. Stumps forming a fairy circle around a solitary trash can.

I fantasize. The trash can is the Round Table—the stumps are chairs for the Knights of the Round. What a stupid fantasy.

It's Christmas Eve morning and everyone's at home, getting ready for Christmas Eve night or whatever. The real Eve. No one's deranged enough to come sit here at this hour. Except, well, me.

Wasn't the Holy Grail all about slaying dragons?

Maybe I've got it wrong. I have to admit—the cultural heritage of Western Europe isn't really my strong suit. I can tell you this, though. I'm no dragon-slayer. It was a lucky dragon—a creature we'd seen on a movie screen—that brought my first girlfriend to me. And this fact, this brilliant fact, has been a factor in my life ever since. Dragons have had a special place in my heart. That in mind, I think I need to reconsider my presence at the Round Table. I'll stand against the Knights if I have to. Yeah, my fantasy's all wrong. I'm on Team Dragon.

I mean, this creature—or creation, whichever—let me read my first girlfriend like a dream.

My ass is freezing.

On this headless stalagmite.

This lifeless piece of stone. Wonder if I can warm it up.

Think warm thoughts.

Pray for warmth.

I'm asleep before I know it.

Christmas Eve morning, in the heart of Odaiba. I start dreaming. Everything that had been swirling around in my head suspends. In my sleep, I can see. A vision. For the first time in a long time, everything's clear—in focus. Almost like the dreams I had when I was ten or eleven. I'm in the dream—the dream world floods my senses.

I wonder if the Japanese language can do justice to my dreams now.

Have I got any better at the language of dreams?

Only one way to find out.

I was in a room. I was there—in the dream. Strange. I could see my own body. My whole body. In the real world, I can't do that. All I can see is my hands, my arms up to my elbows, my belly, my legs. *I'm a character in this world.* Not some viewer, outside of it all. I'm a part of it—under its control.

Seeing my whole body proves it.

In that moment, I'm in that world—that "room".

Everything's fuzzy. The edges blur. What's going on? Take a good look. OK, where am I? At a writing desk. Sitting in an armchair... A cabriolet?

I'm leaning back with all my weight.

And I'm watching myself lean back. So where am I watching from? From what perspective? Hovering just above ground. Almost like a guardian angel, watching over myself.

After a while, the line between my two selves vanishes.

Then—all of a sudden—I'm looking at the "room" through

the eyes in the head of the body in the chair. Leaning back into the cabriolet.

The ceiling hangs low.

It vaults... Or curves? I need to check it out. I spin around—I guess this cabriolet can spin. Or maybe it's not a cabriolet.

There's a bed across from the writing desk. A single (not a twin, not a double). The linens are fresh, unwrinkled. The work of professionals, no doubt. At the head of the bed, by the headboard, the ceiling curves down the wall.

I get up to take a closer look. No wall. It's like the ceiling goes down to the floor. (Down to the headboard?) There's a window there. Covered by curtains. The curtains are thick— like shrouds. I reach out to touch them. They feel smooth, like curtains should. I pull them back to find another set of curtains. Lace, this time.

Behind that?

Just darkness.

I feel beyond the lace. There's nothing outside this window. I pull back the second set of curtains. The window's boarded up. Nothing to see.

That sort of thing normally scares the shit out of me. But, in the dream, I have no fear.

OK, the bedside window's no good. What about the others? Where are the others?

I take a look around the "room". Nothing else you could call a window.

Ceiling, wall, floor. That's pretty much it.

What is this place?

A hotel, I bet. What else could it be?

Over time, the "room" takes the shape of a room. But there's no wall by the bed. That stays the same. The slope is like the nose of a bullet train. I go back to the writing desk, but don't sit down. I look at the desk. Something's off. Way off. Dust—the desk is covered in two or three centimetres of dust. What gives?

On the right side of the table, there's a TV. Under that, a cabinet. On wheels. Wait—maybe it's not a cabinet. More like a safe. (The longer I stare at it, the more it starts looking like a safe.) It's got a sticker on it. There's some writing on it. A clue? Instructions? It looks like instructions—like how to use a life jacket or something. For emergencies, like if there's a fire in the hotel—to escape. There's something written in Japanese.

It says: OPEN ONLY IN EMERGENCY. Then there's an inspection date and a signature.

There's more writing. Besides the Japanese. English and... Chinese? The characters look like the *kanji* I know, but different. Simplified Chinese? I can read some, not others. Not sure what it says.

I look back at the desk and the dust is even thicker now. I brush it off.

Then I see it. There's a CD. Didn't expect that. How thin is this case? I feel like a forty-niner discovering gold dust. I take the CD in my hands—lovingly.

It has a yellow jacket. There's a black man on the cover, holding a tenor sax. "Sonny Rollins with the Modern Jazz Quartet." Is that the title? Band name? Both?

Sonny Rollins.

I flip the case over. Thirteen tracks in all. "The Stopper", "Shadrack", "On a Slow Boat to China".

That's where I wake up.

Violently.

I'm cut out of the picture. The dream spits me out.

I'm shaking. From the cold. Back on my stone stump in the middle of Symbol Promenade Park.

CHRONICLE
—1985—

We age, but we're not alone. The same goes for our city. So—how has Tokyo got older? How has it grown up? These are the kinds of questions we'll tackle in "Tokyo Chronicle", a new series launching in our next issue.

In the meantime, here's a little taste of what we've got in store—a teaser, if you will. Kaku Nohara kicks things off with a short story about his Tokyo, circa 1985. Before we get to his story, just a few lines about where the world was in 1985.

AIDS landed in Japan. Gorbachev was picked to succeed Chernenko. Aug. 15: PM Yasuhiro Nakasone paid a visit to Yasukuni Shrine, in an official capacity. Race riots raged in South Africa. Japan Airlines flight 123 crashed near Mt. Osutaka, Gunma Prefecture. In Ibaraki, EXPO Tsukuba 1985 ran for 184 days. The New Entertainment Control Law went into effect. Oct. 16: Hanshin Tigers named Central League champions.

THE PEPSI WARS
By Kaku Nohara

We're all ten years old. Old enough to taste the difference. And you can buy Coke at any convenience store... Really, where's the fun in that? We're on the hunt for Pepsi-Cola.

Pepsi's different. Premium. A rare brew manufactured in underground power stations.

I issue the order:

—Fall in!

We're in West Shinjuku. The quiet second district. Quiet—because the 1.569 billion-yen Tokyo Metropolitan Government Office hasn't gone up yet. We assemble by the Water Plaza in Central Park, our base of operations.

—Uno

—Dos

—Tres

—Cuatro

—Sinkhole

Our secret code.

I'm the commander, so I take the lead: Got your timepieces, amigos?

All at once: Si, señor!

Yuji Okazaki spent the summer in Spain with his family. When he came back, Spanish hit us hard—at an instantaneous wind speed of fifty metres per second.

Me: Ready? Synchronize watches. You have exactly five minutes. And no Fanta—got it? Pepsi only.

Hiroki Uehara (raising his hand): Are vending machines out of bounds?

Me: Affirmative. Stores only. Clear? Get receipts, too—for evidence. Everyone reading twelve seconds?

All of us: Yessir!

Me: Ready... get set... go!

We run like hell.

We hit every Pepsi-carrying store we can find. Pepsi. Rocket fuel for the double-digit generation.

Hopped up on caffeine, we barrel through the streets of Shinjuku. As I bolt towards the next store, I catch a glimpse of the Tokyo Hilton. Or should I say El Hilton? Remember, though, the H is silent.

That was my 1985.

BOAT FOUR
NO WAY OUT

I never was much of a talker, but after that ill-fated car chase—when I lost my first girlfriend—I really clammed up. Let my fists do all the talking. I lashed out at everyone in range: the adults trying to hold me back, the other kids at The End of the World, everybody, anybody. Third grade, eighth grade, it made no difference to me. Then they sent me home to Suginami, supposedly rehabilitated.

Back to school.

As soon as I saw all those ugly faces for the first time in a year, I got kind of slap-happy.

I'm pretty sure I took a swing at every kid in my grade before the semester was up. I mean it. In the spirit of being open and honest, there's something I need to admit. I didn't spare girls. It was low of me, I know, but on average, they were the better fighters.

We beat each other senseless. All of us. There was plenty of hate to go around. "Peaceful resolution"? Huh? What's that even mean? Peace is just a ruse. Granted, "ruse" wasn't in my vocabulary back then. But I felt it in my bones. We all did. All rise, bow—and come out swinging!

In no time, I was slapped with a bad rep. I made it into middle school, but Suginami ward put me on blast. *I was an ex-dropout who hit girls.* Blacklisted. In middle school, likes and loves were flying all over the place. Boys and girls and unchained libidos. But I played no part in the adolescent melodrama. I was hanging out in my corner, alone, giving off bad vibes.

High school was easier on me. All boys. No girls meant no girls to hit.

But my school wasn't easier on everyone. During my time there, three boys (in different grades) killed themselves, one kid in my grade survived a family suicide, and another kid murdered his parents in their sleep. (He doused his house in gasoline and set it on fire.)

The rash of deaths didn't have anything to do with my school, though, not really. Every school has kids who want to kill themselves, and kids who want to kill their parents, and parents who want to kill their kids. But the media likes to find patterns where there aren't any. FIVE TRAGEDIES IN THREE YEARS—WHAT'S WRONG WITH THIS SCHOOL? There were talk shows about us, dramatizations, you name it. Our school was legendary. Every time I turned on the TV, I was back in school. It was crazy.

This school stood for everything wrong with the Japanese education system. Wild kids = wild homes = the end of Japan as we know it. Like that.

TV crews were always hanging around. We knew exactly what they wanted to hear—and we delivered. STUDENTS SPEAK UP—TEENAGERS AT THE END OF THE CENTURY.

We were in magazines and newspapers. We were even on TV. As unpaid extras.

The more over-the-top we were, the more they ate it up. Even though every word out of our mouths was pure bullshit.

We worked on our story, transforming an unexceptional boys' school into the campus of the damned. People were afraid of us—even lowlifes from schools way worse than ours didn't dare mess with us. That felt real good.

We felt something like school pride.

We invented a kind of language of our own. Words that fitted our own needs. *Japanese for idiots*, or something. For the first time in years, language made some sense to me. That was when I started speaking up—almost like a regular kid. Like I was part of something.

Sure, that camaraderie had its limits. Our language didn't exist outside of the school and its immediate surroundings. And it didn't last long. But it got us through some strange times.

Years later, I bumped into one of my classmates, but everything was different. When high school ended, that world ended. Everyone went their separate ways. Me? I went the way of the proper young gentleman. If you can believe: I studied liberal arts at a private university. No joke.

That came with a different circle of friends.

Boys *and* girls.

University. It didn't take long to have a few close encounters with girls. But these girls were nothing like my first girlfriend. I mean, I wouldn't call them "girlfriends". More like science experiments. What happens when you introduce manganese dioxide to hydrogen peroxide? Oxygen! When ammonia and hydrochloric acid combine, you get... white smoke! Don't try this at home, kids! *Ha ha ha*. Yeah, like that's gonna happen.

University.

School, sex, bar, school, work, double date ("collaborative research"), mid-terms, sex.

Science, it turns out, can be pretty medieval. Look at alchemy, the magic of converting base metals into gold. What am I trying to say? Love can lead to sex—of course. But there are times when things go the other way around. Sex can lead to love. That's what I'm saying. I know it can happen because it happened to me. How many times? Well, just once.

I was nineteen.

And she was nineteen.

A bunch of us from class went out for drinks. We drank, a lot, then staggered over to her place. The couples among us vanished as the witching hour approached. Only four of us—two girls, this girl and me—stayed over, drinking and talking through the night. But as the night went on, the two girls started saying: "I gotta go home," and "Shitshitshit, I need to get my books from my room," and "Omigod, my hair is a total mess." They left as soon as trains started running again in the morning. And then there were two. We said we were tired or cold or whatever—then got under the covers of her narrow single bed. We got good and close. I got a hard-on, then the thing that had to happen happened.

Within a half-hour, we'd finished—twice. Our chemistry was incredible. Explosive.

We sat up at the head and foot of her bed and looked at each other. For real this time. Starting over. "Nice to meet you."

We're buck-naked.

Me: We've had class together—what—twice?

Her: Three times, I think.

Me: Really? Already?

Her: Did you skip one?

Me: I dunno. Maybe.

Her: What do you want to do for breakfast?

Me: Go to the station?

Her: The... station?

Me: At this hour, the soba stall's probably the best bet.

Her apartment was in Komagome, at the end of the shopping district. It was a five-minute walk from the JR station. That's right, JR. It was now Japan Railways. National Railways was a thing of the past. Because when she and I were nineteen, the world was 1994.

19-19-1994.

Sounds ominous. Like an emergency phone number you hope you never have to call.

We spent the next few months lost in sex. Somewhere in there, she became my girlfriend—the second to appear in my history. Long live poverty! Every girl I'd ever been involved with commuted from home—somewhere in the twenty-three wards of Tokyo. And the same went for me.

A pure Suginami boy. When I needed privacy, I had to buy it. Most of the time, that meant love hotels. Karaoke boxes weren't made for going all the way. But asking a girl to go fifty-fifty on a love hotel was basically impossible. In other words, "dating" tended to eat up what little money I had.

Until then.

Until her.

We did it whenever we felt like it. Because she had her own place. Her bed was ours to use however we wanted. We made it creak, we made it shake. That's how we got closer—by getting physical. We were making something. Alchemically, I mean.

She was from way up north. Asahikawa, Hokkaido.

And she, by the way, had these amazing areolae, like, around her nipples. I'm a breast guy. I love breasts. But hers were special—unlike any I've ever seen. Just the shape of them—they had *purpose*.

"See this?" she asked, showing me her left breast while we were in bed. "Looks like Hokkaido, right?"

"Holy shit... Yeah."

Without a doubt, her left areola was a flawless map of Hokkaido.

Complete with the Habomai Islands.

For the record, she called them her "areas"—not areola. A little too generic for my taste.

"Here are the Tokachi Plains," she pointed, giving me the full tour. "... And here's where I come from. The middle of the Kamikawa Basin. No, not there! That's my nipple... See where the skin dips in? That's the Ishikari River. Sapporo's over here..."

"Cool, cool."

"OK, pop quiz—where's Hakodate?"

"Um, around here?"

"Gold star! You really know your geography. I don't know where anything is around Tokyo."

"God, you've got such excellent areolae. The more I look, the more I like."

"Right? I'm really proud of my areas."

"You mean... you show them to people?"

"Why? Are you jealous? Haha."

That was how we loved each other.

"I had to come to school in Tokyo," she tells me, "to break free from Hokkaido."

She's cursed, she says. A conclusion reached after eighteen years. Her fate was tied to her birth island. Hokkaido.

"Well, did it work? Do you feel free?"

"Not yet," she says. "Take a look over here."

From left to right. She directs my attention to the areola on her other breast.

This one was no less meaningful. It was just—I dunno—more *geometric*. A shape nothing like Hokkaido.

"If the left one's Hokkaido," she tells me, "then this one's got to be someplace, too."

"So," I say, "if the one on the left is where you're from..."

She cuts in: "... then the one on the right is where I'm supposed to go."

"Yeah, the place where you'll find peace and happiness. Your Shangri-La. So your areolae are like a map of your life."

"Totally. I need to find this place... If I don't find it, I'll never break the curse, right? If I can't find it, then there's no way out—you know what I mean?"

It made perfect sense to me. So we started searching. For a place in the shape of the excellent areola on her right breast.

When I shut my eyes, I can see its outline perfectly.

Even now.

We had no money. So our dates were pretty much limited to the Komagome neighbourhood. Rikugien Park was our favourite spot. When we had no classes and no plans, we'd spend the whole day there—enjoying what the pamphlet bills as "one of the most beautiful places in Tokyo". We got there at opening and stayed until they closed at five. Even admission stung a little, so we never splurged on the in-park teahouse or anything. We packed our own refreshments. Du Zhong tea poured into water bottles. We woke up at eight to make our own lunches. Some days, "lunch" was a couple of rice balls. Like I said, we were broke.

But we were perfectly happy.

It got us giddy just watching the big-mouthed carp swimming in the pond.

Walking around the park always got us worked up. So we went at it—in the darker parts of the park. Hidden behind trees, out of sight. Sometimes we did our best to keep quiet. Sometimes we didn't.

Cut us some slack. We were nineteen.

Our search for the mystery land mass mapped on her right breast went on. Whenever we found time (i.e., when we weren't busy getting busy), we would hit the library or the bookstore. We'd look through travel books or spin globes in hopes of finding the place where she belonged. We even read anthropology articles, but nothing was panning out. We didn't give up, though. Shangri-La was out there somewhere, waiting to be found.

We put on our thinking caps.

If Hokkaido's cold, maybe this other place is warm—even tropical? So our eyes gravitated towards equatorial regions. We gave the Caribbean a good look. We studied the rigid borders on the African continent—lines left over from the colonial age. We kept an eye on the seas that had the most islands, the area between Indonesia and the Philippines, the Aegean Sea. Come to find out, though, the Aegean can actually get pretty chilly.

Alas, it's darkest at the foot of the lighthouse. A saying meant just for us, it seems. It was July 1994. Mid-terms were probably over already. I ran into a classmate somewhere on campus—and he had all these geography books out on the table. Not college texts... more like supplementary material for middle-school texts. "For use with *New Geography* (Tokyo Publishing) or *Our Society—An Introduction to Geography* (Japan Books)." That sort of thing.

"What's going on? Are you tutoring kids or something?" I think I asked.

"Uh-huh. I signed up with an agency. They find jobs for me."

"Did they charge a lot?"

"Not that much. I get a lot of work, so it was totally worth it."

"Cool."

That was pretty much our whole conversation.

My girlfriend was there, too, quietly thumbing through those geography books, as if taking a trip down memory lane. She went through a set of flash cards of "Japan's 47 Prefectures". Chock-full of handy statistics: co-ordinates, population, resources, climate, etc. She lingered on the last of the forty-seven, Okinawa, just sort of hovering there. Then she said something.

Not words, really. If I had to write it down, I'd go with something like: *N-mwah!*

Me: Whatwhat?

Her: This.

She had her finger on it. This funny triangle, sort of in the middle of the ocean... Holy shit! It looked exactly like the one on her right breast. Miyakojima.

One of the islands of Okinawa (formerly the Kingdom of Ryukyu).

Unbelievable.

She'd found the other shape. On the left, Hokkaido. On the right, Miyakojima.

Her areolar oracle had been revealed in full.

It was in Japan all along. Talk about a serious short circuit. We'd been blind—hyperopic, at least. What made us so sure that her Shangri-La *wasn't* in Japan? Another misreading in my life of misreadings.

In that moment, we understood. Setting foot on Miyako-jima was the goal—the way out. But this story is a little longer than that, so bear with me.

Her: I need money for the flight.

Me: Right, of course.

Her: But that's it, right?

Me: Guess so.

Her: Like, I need money for food and a room. But that won't be a problem—as long as I get a job.

Me: And, like, stay there a while?

Her (looking into the distance): What's stopping me? I mean, it's Japan. I don't need a passport. I don't need a work visa.

Me: But what about school?

Her: First things first. My Promised Land awaits!

Fair enough.

If this was a kabuki play, this would be the place where the wooden clappers get faster and faster. Things were really moving now. All we needed was 20,000 yen each. We didn't really think about questions like *when* or *how long* (i.e., winter break or spring break?). For the time being, all we needed was capital.

We started job-hunting. Easy enough. Campus was full of flyers for "short-term high-income employment opportunities". They all looked like menus from subpar family restaurants. I weighed a few options before signing up with a security company that had me waving a blinking orange stick—directing traffic around construction sites.

She was looking at the same flyers, but ended up, through

a friend, scoring a plum job at a beach snack bar. Somewhere on the Boso Peninsula, on the side that looks at Tokyo Bay.

The summer before that—summer 1993—was unseasonably cold. Like, record lows. Crops were lost, meaning rice shortages, and the Heisei Rice Riots. Nobody was rushing to the beach. Boso Peninsula was empty, like a ski resort in a snowless winter. But that was 1993. This summer—1994— was ultra-hot. Forty-year highs. Tokyo hit 39.1 degrees in August. HOTTEST DAY SINCE WWII. Air conditioners were selling like hot cakes... And keeping cool was serious business.

"The beach is *waaaaay* packed," she said after her third or fourth day. "It's insane."

Why are my summers always cursed? I guess I should be grateful that my fifth-grade summer died suddenly and didn't drag on forever. This time around, summer was endless. And ruthless. University classes were slated to start in mid-September, and her beach gig was supposed to wrap up by the end of August. That gave us a couple of weeks in between, for ourselves. That's why I put up with it.

With the reality that we couldn't just be together whenever we wanted, not now.

We'd discovered the undeniable truth that making money means selling time. Selling time means time apart. Her bed was no longer Aladdin's magic carpet—always good for a shag. We tried to make things work. After my job, I'd go right to her place in Komagome. Let myself in, wait for her.

But Boso isn't exactly close. It's in the next prefecture. I'm pretty sure she had to change trains at Tokyo Station to get there. She had to be there really early to open up. Sometimes she stayed late to spend time with co-workers, too. At first, it was hard to pin down when she was coming home. After a little while, though, she stopped coming back at all. She started staying with a girl she knew in Chiba.

"If I head back now, there's no way I'll make it to work tomorrow morning..."

Says the voice on the other end of the line.

But why am I playing the obedient husband? Alone in her apartment, waiting for the phone to ring.

Then the thing that had to happen happened.

But wait. Not yet. I have a confession to make. I need to be honest. I was hardly innocent myself. I made my own mistakes. With a twenty-something female security guard from work. I mean, she was friendly. And we... got friendly. Not just once. Four times—no more. "Four", by the way, doesn't reflect the number of times in a single night. Saying "she seduced me" wouldn't be completely honest either. Sex was in the air. In the workplace. And good luck curbing the sexual urges of a nineteen-year-old male.

At first, I just acted cool—like she'd never find out. And she wouldn't. The two of them lived in different worlds.

There was zero chance of them crossing paths.

But that doesn't mean I got off scot-free.

Something I've noticed: whatever happens to me happens to those around me. She was hard at work at the beach—and, just like that, two weeks had gone by without us sharing a sack. There was one time we got close, except: "I'm on my period." Fact is, she was barely ever at Casa Komagome at this point. Really, I should have been paying the rent. Then it hit me: *What if she's sleeping with someone else?* Where did that suspicion come from? From my own indiscretions, obviously. That's what got me thinking.

Thinking? More like I was consumed by jealousy.

But I tried to hide it. I mean, I had no proof—and, more to the point, I had no right.

I wanted to be optimistic. Like, if something's going on, maybe it's just meaningless sex... right?

Crap, this sucks.

I had a pretty good guess who the mystery lover might be. "Yakisoba Man". A local surfer she worked with. He was older than her (older than *us*, I guess...), and apparently he could fry noodles like nobody else. The second I heard about this dude, something didn't sit right. I mean, he's too healthy—a healthy mind in a healthy body. Nothing like me. I'd never touched a surfboard, and instant ramen was the fullest extent of my noodle abilities. Don't get me wrong, I have some pretty strong feelings about Peyoung sauce, but I couldn't compete with this motherfucker.

I break the news to myself: "Listen, man, chances are good she's sleeping with Yakisoba Man."

"I see. Is it fatal?"

"No," I tell myself. "Because I love her."

I won't push it, I can't. It's just temporary. It'll end when Boso closes. Things can go back to the way they were—our love is strong. As long as I don't blow it now. September will make everything right. We'll be back in our honeymoon suite in Komagome. I mean, Yakisoba Man's geographically out of range—he lives in *Chiba*. So I keep my mouth shut and wait for the tide to turn.

But that didn't happen. September rolled around, and she was still hanging out in Boso, not coming home at night.

I think it was a few days into the month—maybe a week?

This memory has no *when*. I know. On some subconscious level, I want to forget, right? Some complex? Some deep desire? But I definitely remember where I was. In the apartment in Komagome. Her apartment—but she's not there. I'm waiting for her. Waiting for that ominous sound.

The phone rings.

Twice. Then it stops. Then it starts again.

I pick up. "Hello?"

It's her. "I'm at Haneda..."

I can hear the roar of Tokyo International Airport in the background. She's on a payphone, calling her home phone—calling me.

"I got two tickets for Okinawa," she says. She doesn't wait for me to say anything back. "Two tickets to leave Haneda, touch down in Naha, then fly over to Miyakojima. You understand what I'm saying?"

"I–I think so."

"No, you don't—you don't know if the extra ticket's yours. I don't even know... My job at the beach is over. I guess it's been over for a while. I've got the money now, and I'm ready to leave. I can even cover a room for two. So... I'm going to Miyakojima. Myself plus one."

"Plus me?"

"I don't know..."

"What do you mean?"

"I need to make the same call to someone else."

I say nothing.

She doesn't ask me to come.

She tells me her flight number. Tells me her departure time. Says she'll be waiting by the airline counter.

There isn't much time.

"I can't make this choice alone," she says. The noise of the terminal nearly drowns her out. She sounds a little hoarse, but I can't be sure. "So you have to choose for me. You have to choose me. If you drop everything and come with me, the ticket's yours. If you can't choose me, then I can't choose you."

Silence. That's it?

No explicit mention of Yakisoba Man.

"I'm getting on this plane—I'm leaving Tokyo," she says, "and I want *someone* to come with me..."

The call ends with a soft click.

Then total silence.

BEEP BEEP BEEP BEEP—the alarm in my brain is screaming again. I'm fully alert. I decide. I choose her. There's no need to overthink it. I love her, and everyone fucks up, right? I mean, I fucked up. Right?

If I run as fast as I can, I can get to the station in under a minute and a half.

Save that seat for me.

Komagome Station is on the Yamanote Loop Line—so I'll take the Yamanote to Hamamatsucho, then grab the monorail to Haneda. But first things first. The Yamanote is a circle—so which way gets me there faster? Something tells me to go with the outside loop, towards Tokyo Station. I don't count stops or anything. I just listen to my bones.

But something's wrong at Komagome Station. I hear the announcements, but I can't get a good read on the situation. All I know is that there's a situation. OK, they're saying something about "the power grid". Outside loop's down. Down how? How down? I map the Yamanote in my head. The dot for Komagome rests near the northern edge of the circle—Hamamatsucho is towards the south-east. (Counting stations after the fact: Hamamatsucho is twelve stops from Komagome on the outside loop—seventeen stops on the inside.)

OK. Change of plans. The inside loop's still running, so I'll take the loop the other way. I've already lost several stations' time—gotta fly.

The train shows up, and it's packed. Full of people who got turned around, like me. Therein lies the beauty of the loop—it's a simple detour, go the other way. I force my way onto the train. It leaves Komagome, making brief stops at Sugamo, Otsuka, Ikebukuro. Then, a few hundred metres shy of the Mejiro platform, the train grinds to a halt. I didn't know about the guerrilla attacks on Tokyo's power stations. That information wasn't available on the trains. No one had a cell phone—*because the train was stuck in 1994.* "Synchronized attacks," the media would call it the next morning. What the fuck, extremists? Now my train's stranded between Ikebukuro and Mejiro—the most distant point on the loop from where I need to be. Well, shit. Even the air conditioner is out of commission—in this record heat. The train was hot to begin with, and overcrowded—we're all dripping with sweat. I hear a beat, leaking out of someone's headphones. *Tick-tick, tick-tick. Tick-tick, tick-tick.* Almost like a time bomb about to explode.

A time bomb inside of me.

In this heat, we're all an inch from losing our shit.

An announcement comes over the speaker. The conductor levels with us: *We don't know when we're going to be moving again. Please stay calm.*

And that's when I lose it. "I want to get off!" I scream.

Within a couple of seconds, everyone else loses it too: "So what!" "Suck it up!"

You don't understand, I say. If this train doesn't start moving, I'll miss my flight. I'll never get out of Tokyo. I'll lose my girlfriend. So—"OPEN THAT FUCKING DOOR! LET ME THROUGH—I'LL OPEN IT MYSELF."

They try to stop me as I struggle towards the door:

"THE TRAIN WON'T MOVE IF THE DOORS ARE OPEN!"

"DON'T TOUCH THAT FUCKING DOOR!"

But justice is on my side. "MOVE," I demand. And I push. "I'M GETTING OUTTA HERE." If I can get off this dead train, I can get a taxi on Mejiro Avenue, or hightail it to Takadanobaba and take the subway. It's not too late. I can still reach her. So—"OUTTA MY WAY, ASSHOLES!"

I start elbowing, pushing, throwing punches. But the whole train's seething with rage. When I let my fists fly, fists come flying right back. The harder I hit, the harder I get hit. Action and reaction. I started it. And now they're ending it.

I'm knocked down, beat up, blacked out.

Yeah... No way out.

BOAT FIVE
ALMOST LIKE PERPETUAL MOTION

Doesn't look like rain's coming after all. My prophecy: *Christmas Eve, 2002. You shall not know rain.* Then the dark sky looks down on me, taunts me. That's right. Feel the cold—feel it all over. Can't you see what's coming? I'm still trembling like I was before.

I make my way over Teleport Bridge. On one side, Tokyo Teleport Station on the Rinkai Line. On the other, Odaiba Seaside Park Station on the Yurikamome Line.

It was ten minutes to noon when I woke up on my stalagmite. Meaning I was out for a good two hours. That long? Something's definitely calling to me. But it's not time yet. That's why the dream cut me out.

Let the memories come. Let them dig in.

Think archaeologically.

I'm standing in front of DECKS Tokyo Beach. Not a real beach. It's a building made to look like a cruise liner, but it looks more like a ghost ship to me. Time for a little detour. What does Odaiba look like to you? A resort? A glimpse of the near future? A celebrity hotspot? All those images crumble before me as I make my way up the coastline.

I head towards Rainbow Bridge. I follow Shuto Expressway 11 as it veers to the left.

I step into Daiba Park.

Look. This is where Tokyo ends.

The park sits just a few metres above sea level—on a stone-wall embankment. *This is the third daiba.* There used to be six. No. 3 and no. 6 are the only ones left. What's a *daiba*, you ask? An artillery battery built for coastal defence in the late Edo period. To keep the Black Ships at bay. Construction began in the summer of 1853, when Commodore Perry sailed into Uraga. All six *daiba* were ready for action within a year and three months.

Six stations with cannon. That's what "Odaiba" means. See? Fuji TV wasn't Odaiba's first station.

This is the front line. On the waterfront. Man-made stations for defending Edo—the city that became Tokyo.

Daiba 1-10, Minato ward. The present address for the third *daiba*.

Black pines stand on the bank, continuing their meaningless guard. They sway in the wind and shadow—just like they have since the Edo period. Behind the trees: the remains of a barracks, a few ammunition stores. Other traces of war: anti-aircraft guns. (Or "high-angle guns", depending on who you ask... The army and navy had different names for them. Fucking idiots. Looks like the Japanese have been the Japanese at every point in history.) A story forms in my head. That all of this is left over from the Pacific War. Odaiba's *daiba* remanned. Back to your stations, men—America's coming back.

The front line comes back to life. To defend Tokyo once again.

Tokyo's history is called to arms. It comes in waves.
And my own history—it's the same story.
The smell of salt hits me. Shards of memory pierce me.
They dig into me.

And my train fails to arrive at its destination.

I leave the third *daiba* and get on the Yurikamome Line.
Aim for Shinbashi Station, the end of the line. But I'm
freezing-cold, so I stay on the train, where the heater is. We
cross Rainbow Bridge, but I'm too cold to lift my head up to
look for the sixth *daiba*, adrift in the sea below. I curl up like
a ball. To warm up. My brain is moving now—set in motion
by unearthed memories. I draw a map inside my head.
Almost like I did with the Yamanote Line when I was nineteen. But, this time, I chart the flight of the Yurikamome.
The elevated track traces the shape of Odaiba—like a giant
U turned on its side. To the north-west, the line crosses
Rainbow Bridge, then circles around. It forms a head. The
800-metre bridge is like a long neck. Making the sideways
U... a body? Ariake has to be the tail. A dragon's tail? The
second I see the dragon shape in my mind, I fall asleep.

I *fall*. Suddenly into sleep.

The automated train pulls into Shinbashi Station, stops
there for a few minutes, then heads back to Ariake again.
But I don't wake up—because I'm already somewhere else.

There. In that dream.

Back in that "room".

The one in my memories. That hotel room. I wake up
same as last time. *I wake up as a character in that world.* Am

I seeing things from the same angle? Just off the ground? Hard to say. But I'm back in that cabriolet, same as last time. It feels like I'm living the scene over and over.

It feels the same—but it's not.

Last time, I was leaning back in the chair. This time, I'm leaning forward. Like I was when I fell asleep on the train. Like... like I broke through the wall just like that. The thick wall that divides reality and dreams.

Channel your senses, I tell myself. Get a good look at the place.

This world. This "room".

Where's the CD? Back on the desk—like last time?

I know it's important. I can feel it in my bones. I train my eyes, and there it is. The yellow jacket. The man with the saxophone: Sonny Rollins. The dust is thicker now—like the volume's been turned up. *Is time moving?* Is the "room" getting older? I grab the CD from under the dust. Déjà vu. I take the dream's generous gift in my hands. I'm surprised by how thin the case is—same as last time.

I flip it over. White letters on black background. Same thirteen tracks as before. In the same order—at least I think so. Which means, I reason, this CD really exists. It still begins with "The Stopper" and closes with "I Know". But only one track jumps out at me (even though I don't know why—not yet). It's the same one that brought me back from sleep on the stalagmite. "On a Slow Boat to China". It overpowers the other titles—all of which begin to blur.

"On a Slow Boat to China".

I let the words sink in. "Slow", "Boat", "China". Right—I can feel the story they're making. That's what pulls me in.

I get out of the chair.

Where am I?

Look around.

There are parts of the "room" I still haven't seen. Like, where's the door? And where's the bathroom? They have to be around here somewhere, right? Over here? Beyond the left side of the desk—a carpeted hallway. This new part of the "room" comes into focus. I see the door. I head right for it. I want to open it and get out of this place...

I grip the knob, but it won't move.

It's like a wall made to look like a door. Like a fake door. Is it fake?

Maybe. But it won't get me down. I had a feeling it wouldn't be that easy. *My history is called up.* I've known doors like this before. Doors I tried to open—only to be yanked back, beaten senseless. My past knows what the future holds. It asks: *What if the door won't open? Are you gonna lose your shit?*

Nope. I tell myself: *This isn't the way out.* Calmly.

I don't have any emotions in the dream.

The bathroom's next to the door. I take a look inside. Tiny. The shower curtain has lost most of its colour, like the dull coat of an old lion. There's the toilet. Lid down. Next to that, the sink. The mirror is murky. I can't even see my own reflection.

A sign by the faucet, written in red: DON'T WASTE PRECIOUS WATER.

I turn to head back to the desk, but—right when I turn around—I can see that something's changed. Something small, but significant. On the other side of the chair, there's a round table that I'm sure wasn't there before. I get closer. There's an ashtray on top. Full of dust—no butts.

I don't smoke.

This is a weird table. It's weirdly low... and the legs are screwed to the floor. To keep it from moving.

Looks like neither of us are going anywhere.

All of a sudden I feel tired, so I lie down on the bed. I'm looking down at my feet when I feel it. The vibrations. What's shaking? The floor? Maybe the bed? It's constant—but without rhythm. Almost like perpetual motion.

No, it's not the bed. Not *just* the bed.

Everything's vibrating now. The ceiling, the walls, the floor. The "room".

Or maybe it was always vibrating. Maybe I just didn't notice.

I look up at the ceiling.

Is this place really a hotel? Whatever this "room" belongs to. Whatever it is, it feels like it's changing. Because I caught on.

It's forming. I can feel it.

That's where I wake up.

I wake up.

The train is about to arrive at yet another final stop— Ariake Station. I don't see any other passengers around. I try to get my bearings, but I have a hard time wrapping my head around falling asleep in a dream and waking up in "reality".

I'm not shaking any more. Thanks to the heater.

Maybe I'm still forming, too.

But what does *that* mean?

CHRONICLE
—1994—

A homeless girl on TV dared us to give her money. May 9: Mandela was named President of South Africa. "The Surgeon's Photo" of the Loch Ness monster was revealed to be a hoax—sixty years after the fact. In Matsumoto City, Nagano Prefecture, eight people were killed by an unidentified gas. Kansai International Airport opened on a man-made island in the Seto Inland Sea. Sept. 20: Ichiro (playing for the Orix Blue Wave) notched his 200th hit of the season.

THE TROPIC OF CAPRICORN
(OR "THE END OF THE LINE")
By Kaku Nohara

In the end, it was the underground loop. The Marunouchi Line.

Our Tropic of Capricorn. The line the sun hangs over on the winter solstice.

Masuo Hashiguchi poses the question: "Where's our Tropic of Capricorn?"

I answer: "Has to be the line where we dump our trash."

"Huh?"

"Think about it. Yotsuya... Mitsuke..."

Nothing but blank faces.

I take a deep swig of canned coffee (BOSS, to be specific). What a pain to explain. All right—here goes.

The five of us were in college. We spent freshman year drinking and singing and chasing girls. But not sophomore year. We were sick of cheap booze, karaoke was repulsively mainstream and—thanks to semi-permanent girlfriends—our chase was on hold, for the time being.

Shigeru Kaji: High time we found another way to have fun...

Me: High time?

Takeru Igarashi: We're sophomores now. We're in the big time...

Hisashi Iwata: But our girlfriends eat up all our cash.

Me: The price of courtship...

Hashiguchi, Kaji, Igarashi and Iwata all nod.

Shopping was never our bag anyway. So—what else could we do for kicks?

Work. That was the answer to our prayers. Nothing beats short-term employment. You can choose what you want to do, and every workplace comes with its own discoveries (varies from person to person). Best of all, you get paid. Talk about the ideal hobby.

Sophomore year. The five of us landed jobs.

Different jobs doing different things in different places.

But our work hours weren't all that different.

We always met up on the way to work. Mid-commute, in a subway station. At first, our rendezvous was Akasaka Mitsuke Station. It's well connected—it has the Ginza and Marunouchi Lines. I had to get to Honancho on the

Marunouchi Line (switching or not switching trains at Nakano Sakaue). Akasaka Mitsuke was on the way. Pretty much every morning from August to September, we met up in Mitsuke. To share an underground breakfast before heading to work. Proof of our friendship. Whenever a girlfriend prepared something for one of us, we split the spoils five ways.

We were working for fun. It was just a hobby—so we didn't stay in one place for long. We switched jobs at breakneck speed. And when we changed jobs, we changed stations, too. The location changed—but our morning ritual was constant.

When we were done eating, the trash had to go somewhere. But some lines had better trash cans than others. If you ask me, the Marunouchi Line had the best bins in the business.

Masuo Hashiguchi: That's how you think of the Marunouchi Line? The one with the trash cans?

Me: Pretty much.

Hisashi Iwata: Oh.

Shigeru Kaji: I think I get that.

Me: The day before yesterday was the solstice...

We crush our empty coffee cans.

Me (continuing): And I was on the Marunouchi Line— heading to Yotsuya. You know how it's always dark, because you're underground, then right before you get to the station you surface and the sun hits you? The other day, at that moment, I felt like the sun was right over me. Then I got off at Yotsuya and met up with you mugs.

Hisashi Iwata: Oh.

Shigeru Kaji: I get that.

Masuo Hashiguchi: Works for me. Real poetic. I guess I was thinking kind of literally. Like, some tropical location somewhere.

Me: What made you ask anyway?

Masuo Hashiguchi: I dunno. Guess I was daydreaming. About a little getaway, just us and our girlfriends.

Me: In the middle of winter?

Masuo Hashiguchi: Haha, yeah... Like those celebrities who fly to Honolulu for New Year's or something.

Takeru Igarashi: Sign me up, man.

Masuo Hashiguchi: You serious?

Kaji and Iwata and I all nod. Unanimous.

Masuo Hashiguchi: Is it just me... or is it getting hot down here?

The end of the line?

We didn't know our underground breakfasts wouldn't last forever.

We didn't know about the 1995 underground gas attack. Or the citywide removal of subway station trash receptacles that would follow.

A future with nowhere for trash to go.

Nobody saw that coming. Because we were still living in 1994.

BOAT SIX
YOU? IN BUSINESS?

About my third girlfriend.

Fast-forward six years—to 2000 A.D. Except, well, I wasn't some boy in a bubble. Things happened in between. So let me fill you in real quick.

A detour before we get around to my third escape attempt and its inevitable failure.

Remember my rival in love? Yakisoba Man? Well, I thought he was my rival, but I guess that was all in my head. Yakisoba Man never made it to Haneda, either. That's right. My second girlfriend caught that plane to Okinawa, plus none. She was totally devastated when I didn't show. It makes me want to cry out at a hundred decibels: YOU'RE WRONG!

But how could she know? She had no idea I was blacked out on a train on the Yamanote Line. Typically, I'm the great misreader. I like to think I hold the patent on getting things wrong. Shit, I probably could have sued her for patent infringement.

This is what I get for going behind his back...

I bet she was crushed. Clueless and crushed.

She got on that flight (the seat beside her empty), connected in Naha, and landed in Miyakojima.

Did she find Shangri-La there?

Beats me.

I learnt everything I know—her side of the story or whatever—from a letter. One letter from Okinawa. That's all she wrote. My second girlfriend quit school (by the time she sent that letter, the necessary paperwork had already been filed with the admissions office) and vacated Casa Komagome (an aunt from Saitama acted as her proxy), never to return from her areolar paradise.

OK, my turn.

I read that letter in my hospital bed. My mom brought it when she came to visit. Yeah, my heart was broken. But that wasn't the only thing. I was hospitalized for broken bones sustained in the Yamanote brawl. Or, as the episode is known in the annals of my history, TRAGEDY OUTSIDE MEJIRO STATION. All of this **bold**.

My injuries were pretty serious. Three months to recover—that was the diagnosis. After I passed out on the train, men and women of all ages walked all over me, leaving me with six broken ribs. How many were left? On the bright side, my spinal cord was apparently intact.

Things were that bad.

That was how I learnt that when someone blacks out, they really black out.

They beat the shit out of me. No, they beat a lesson into me. *There's no way I'm ever getting out of Tokyo.* Everything went black. Next thing I remember: the white fluorescence of my hospital room. I was looking up at the ceiling above my narrow cot. That was two days after my first procedure.

I was famous. Or—you know—infamous. The other pas- sengers were seeking "damages". Guess they were told to go after JR, too. The charges were, I went off like a machine gun—assaulting innocent after innocent. That was how the newspapers spun it the morning after: SIGN OF THE TIMES—REBEL WITHOUT A COMPASS LASHES OUT DURING GUERRILLA ATTACKS.

Let me get this straight. It was "innocents" who put me in the hospital?

Why the hell should I pay them anything? Isn't that a little extreme?

While I was knocked out, the victims sang their innocent tune. Altogether now: "Money money money money!"

Then the media circus jumps in—singing in a round: "La-la-la logic can go fuck itself! Go fuck itself la-la-la-la."

Justice had left me hard-up.

From my hospital bed, I watched the pile of bills grow. Meanwhile, reporters camped outside my Suginami home and interviewed every housewife in the neighbourhood, asking them what kind of kid they thought would do some- thing so heinous. (My dear neighbours never failed to bring up my dropout past.) Whatever. Who cares?

My mom, it turns out.

"Moron!"

The first word out of her mouth when she came to the hospital.

Then, icy as a freezer: "You're paying for this yourself! Everything. Your hospital bill, whatever you owe the people you swung at in the train. From now on, don't even think about asking me for anything. That means tuition—if your school will even have you back. And once you get out of this bed, you can find your own place to live. You're not coming home. You show your face and the TV crews will never leave. We're going out of our minds dealing with them. Really, what the hell's wrong with you? You're a goddamn train wreck!"

Train wreck... My mom sure has a way with words.

Then what happened?

I worked like a horse—I had debts to pay. I borrowed what I needed to settle up my hospital bills, then paid my "victims" in monthly instalments. I found jobs. Day jobs, night jobs. Sometimes, I had three-shift days: morning, swing and graveyard. Sleep? I wasn't sleeping much, to be honest. On average, I probably got a little over three hours a night. Maybe four. Just enough to keep a body moving. The only thing I had going for me was my youth—the inexhaustible energy of a nineteen-year-old. Nothing else. Just the stamina to fuel me through the sleepless years to follow.

I didn't have time for rest, so I learnt to sleep deep. Quality over quantity. Meaning "no distractions". Everything had to go. Including dreams.

I had almost no dreams in my workhorse years.

Not even enough to fill a short film.

It's really strange. When I was ten or eleven, I did nothing but dream—now I was totally dry.

Life has a way of doing that—restoring balance. That's how I see it, at least.

My mom really did kick me out of the house. I moved into a small, cheap place in Shinjuku. Kami-ochiai, ni-chome. The closest station was Nakai, on the Seibu Shinjuku Line. It was in a two-storey building several decades old. It was all wood, so I guess it had to be built after the war. Shared toilet, no bath. The sort of place where people live when they don't have money—where rent's stuck in the golden age of Godzilla. Financially, I cut every corner I could, spending next to nothing on food, almost never using electricity, never turning on the gas. I streamlined my bathing routine, which involved trips to the local bath and the coin shower (note: three minutes for the price of a coffee). I made it a priority to find jobs where meals were provided—which had the added benefit of helping me balance my diet. Clocking out of my last job for the day, I went straight home and slipped right into bed. No heat, no lights, no nothing. That's how I survived. I didn't have a phone, but my building had a line in the hallway, so I could receive calls from the outside world—as long as somebody was around to pick up. After a couple of years of hardcore work, I bought a PHS. One of my bosses (at a courier company) said I needed to get it, and told me where I could find one for almost nothing. My first briquette of plastic. At long last—the cellular age!

I spent all my time making money. Wages in, damages out. Soon I was twenty—a full-fledged adult. Not that I stopped to celebrate my entry into adult society or anything.

Outside of work, my life was a perfect blank.

My early twenties. Filled with a peace I'd never known. The calm of nearly dropping dead from overwork.

*

Click. The digital calendar flips, the century ends. From 12-31-1999 to 01-01-2000. A whole lot of zeros. Some feared the date. Like the Rapture was upon us. Others celebrated. Couples dying to have "millennium babies" sought pharmaceutical assistance to get the timing just right. Still others, partying in high-end hotel rooms, uncorked ultra-high-end champagne bottles. *Pop, pop, pop.* Even more people burrowed into underground bunkers, waiting to see if the computerized world would descend into anarchy. They really thought that, in one apocalyptic moment, bank accounts would vanish, aircraft would drop out of the sky and nuclear missiles would destroy the planet as we know it. Good old Y2K. The Japanese government didn't help—telling families: "Be sure to stock up on mineral water and emergency food supplies." Panic. Sheer panic. The world was in jeopardy—double jeopardy—whether it was God or computers was inconsequential.

OK, my Y2K. For me, the collapse of the world's banks was the big fear. A matter of life and death, if you think about it. So, on the first of January, I got in line to receive my ATM oracle, like everyone else.

I hadn't bothered checking my balance in years. What's the point, right?

Then my turn came, and—what the hell—did Y2K do this? This couldn't be right.

But it was. I had been too busy working to notice that I had settled my debts... a good eighteen months back. I was in the black. The ATM was showing me a number I never saw coming.

Seven, almost eight, million yen?

That's how I entered the new millennium.

All right. Time to face the music. I'll never make it out of Tokyo. Two massive failures have made that abundantly clear. Guess it's just my fate. But even if it is, I'll have to fight fate on this one. Fight against my shitty karma. Granted, I've been a shitty person. But, as a human being, I've got inalienable rights, right?

At least I have plenty of cash for my third escape attempt.

Let's think this through. Prior experience tells me that any attempt to exit Tokyo ends in violence.

If I can't get out, I'll have to bring *out* in. Enter the Trojan Horse of Tokyo.

My master plan.

I need a fortress—an impenetrable, impregnable lair. My own stronghold right in the heart of the city. A place with the power to keep Tokyo out—an *autonomous region*, if you will. A place to fill with all the music and smells and flavours that Tokyo can't handle. Everything Tokyo can't have. I need a place all my own.

You might call it a business.

I had to do something, right?

To keep on fighting. With everything I had.

Not like I had anything left to lose.

March, 2000 A.D. The Power of Kate opens in Asagaya, Suginami ward.

*

Magazines called Kate a café. In reality, I was going for a place that defied definition; I had no interest in opening a "café"—or any place you're supposed to spell with a cute little accent mark. But why should I care? I had misread the world my whole life. So what if the world misread me back?

All that mattered to me was that Kate had the power to fight against Tokyo. Food and drinks were secondary— just a part of my cover. The Power of Kate. Sounds like a Hollywood romcom, doesn't it?

Where did the name come from?

From life. I needed a name when I submitted the paperwork to the broker. I clearly wrote: "The Power of Hate (temporary)." But some bespectacled pencil-pusher misread my handwriting—and Kate was born. Why was I trying to call my place The Power of Hate? Because I hated the world with every fibre of my being.

Still do.

But OK. The Power of Kate.

A quick rundown on everything that had to happen before opening. Phase I. Get a public health licence (takes one day) and a fire safety certificate (two days). There were free courses for both. Next, apply for a restaurant permit—which takes nearly a month. Put together tons of forms for the tax office. Then burn through loads of cash on equipment. Interior renovations, dishes, recruitment...

My only job was going to be running the place. Not cooking, not serving. So—Phase II.

Cooking: I know a guy. No worries there.

Serving: I track down a few foreign waiters. Easy enough. Phase II is over in no time.

Phase III. Set up thirty or so cockroach traps on the premises. Cleanliness is everything.

Then Kate opens. On the second floor of a renovated home on Nakasugi Avenue. I give the place everything I have—guerrilla warfare against my shitty karma. Not much later, my third girlfriend makes her first appearance in the chronicle of my life.

She came from the east...

But, wait, her brother came first. I met him at a beef-bowl joint. No, not at the counter—behind it. In the kitchen. I'd been working there maybe a couple of months. Night shift. (It was one of those twenty-four-hour places.)

Watching him wrist-deep in the pickles, I had to ask:

"You been at this long? You've got the best pickles in the business."

"Huh?"

I figured he was two or three years older than me. His close-cropped hair made him look a little thuggish.

He stares at me, picks up a loaded dish and hurls it to the floor. *SMASH!* Pickles and broken ceramic pieces everywhere.

"What kind of fuckin' question is that?" he says.

"Wh—what?" I just stand there, stunned.

"Listen to me, you little shit..." He's looking me right in the eye. "I'm not some grunt making fast food by the fucking manual. Got it?"

"Ye—yeah. I got it..."

"Here. Try this, asshole."

He grabs something out of the kitchen fridge. It looks a lot like foie gras. When did he make this? He's been feeding this to the staff? Looks amazing. What is it?

"Angler liver—fresh as fuck."

This ain't no yellowtail.

Angler liver and daikon.

"How is it?"

"..."

"Well?"

"Well... damn."

No other words for this. It's like an ambush of flavour, so good, really good. My taste buds explode. I look at him and say: "*Kaboom!!!*"

"What the hell's that supposed to mean?"

I take another bite. That's answer enough.

He starts explaining: "My family's been making sushi for three generations. My old man taught me Edo-style before I could read... I was a teenage sous-chef... I can make any dish you can name. Get it?"

Pretty sure I got it.

"But..." I say.

"What, you want more?"

"Um, yeah... But..."

"But what?"

"If you're this good, why are you working at some no-name beef-bowl?"

He just looks away, coolly.

"Nowhere else I can go. I've got a record."

"A criminal record?"

"Shut up and eat."

That was the beginning of a deeply satisfying partnership.

From then on, nearly every night, I ate what he made for the staff. Soon *kaboom* wasn't cutting it. I had to find new adjectives. Like *kablam* or *kablooey*. How did he come up with all of his mind-blowing creations?

This has to be what they call "fusion".

He was a perfect fit for Kate. I had him on the phone maybe two seconds after I decided to open a place. It was obvious, right?

The first few months went fantastically. Kate drew in plenty of customers, and they seemed pretty satisfied. I know I was. Kate had a potent mix of exotic spices, a region-free menu and nomadic DJs (who were under explicit instructions to *sound like anything but Tokyo*). To destroy any lingering trace of the city, I covered every surface with giant ferns. In time, the place started to look like *Jurassic Park*—minus all the killer dinos. Most critics raved about the excess of oxygen. They loved Kate. Funny. Kate had been misread again—billed as a café ahead of its time.

It was a hit.

Idiots. Tokyo thought my Trojan Horse was avant-garde? Die, Tokyo, die.

*

So—did my escape plan work?

Well, Kate hit a bit of a speed bump in June. A slipped disc sidelined my chef (the beef-bowl ex-con). "Ca–can't move..." his pained voice hissed through my cell phone. "I'm in the hospital."

"What? Are you OK?"

"Shit no—that's why I'm in the hospital."

"Seriously? What do we do?"

"Man up."

"Huh? You mean like ritual suicide?"

"Yeah, right. Look—Kate has to stay open, with or without me. The doctor has no idea what's wrong. All he does is giggle like a fucking idiot. I can't make any promises about coming back to work. Hate to wuss out like this, but I think I have to hang up my apron."

"CHEF!"

My brain was a total blank.

"Man up, man!"

"Suicide isn't the answer..."

"Knock it off."

Chef was hors de combat, but he was going to make sure Kate stayed open for business. He told me he'd already lined up a replacement, someone he trusted. Nothing for me to do but wait for said help to arrive.

Then help arrived.

It was a few hours later. No introductions, no questions. No "Hello", no "Nice to meet you". She just made a beeline for the kitchen—like she was ready to clock in.

I mean, she didn't look anything like the help I had in

mind. My first thought was: Strange. Kate doesn't get that many high-school girls in uniforms—and they almost never come alone. My second thought was: Isn't it a little hot for a blazer?

That was all I was thinking.

I mean, I thought she was a misguided customer.

"That's the kitchen! You can't—" I start to say.

But the schoolgirl just stares me down. Doesn't say anything.

"You... you can't be back here."

I tried to sound like I was in charge, but—on the inside—all I was thinking was: Hey, she's pretty cute. Piercing eyes. Nice full body.

I guess I was checking her out.

She looks right at me and says sharply:

"Of course I can."

She whips her cell phone out of her skirt pocket and puts it down on the counter like she means business. There's a Snoopy figure dangling from the strap. Then, right in front of me, she starts unbuttoning her blazer. *Pop, pop, pop.* Wh–what is she doing!? She's not gonna show me her boobs or anything!? No. This was no striptease. Not even close.

She opens her blazer to reveal four streaks of metal in the lining—two on each side. Knives.

"My brother says I'm running this kitchen—starting tonight."

"Say what?"

"Don't worry," she says with a smile.

Holy shit, she's cute.

"Just leave everything to me."

Then she heads over to the vegetable stash, grabs a long white daikon and gets to work—reducing it to ultra-thin slices at superhuman speed. *Sssh-sssh-sssh*. Then, *ch-ch-ch-ch-chop*. She fills a bowl with water to soak the diaphanous strands.

I'm speechless.

What skill. No movement is wasted.

A sight to behold.

Then, with a cool look that says *this is nothing*, she turns to me and says:

"You look like you've never seen a teenage knife girl before..."

Another smile.

I was in love.

With my chef's little sister. She moved into her brother's apartment in Koenji that day. Her folks lived in Hatchobori—a neighbourhood for low-level officials... in, like, the Edo period? Everything happened so fast. Mere hours after my chef's untimely injury, she was by his side at the hospital. (She had to be initiated into the mysteries of her brother's menu before making her appearance at Kate.) Living in Koenji made it easy for her to go see him—to drop off fresh clothes, pick up dirty laundry, or ask for help with his more esoteric dishes. Chef's back problems turned out to be pretty serious—just like he predicted. He was discharged after about two weeks, but he was basically an invalid. Whenever his sister wasn't at school or on the job, she did the work of a live-in nurse.

What a sister.

All they had was each other.

"No, my dad's alive," she says one night. She'd just fin-ished making dinner for the staff.

"He is?" I ask, taking my first bite.

My taste buds go wild for her Kyoto-style sablefish. The others love it, too. The Hindu inhales his helping; the Taoist is literally tearing up; the Romanian Christian cuts his fish neatly, then puts it away with the silence of the Black Sea.

"Yeah, he's alive but... Hmph!"

What? What is that? Hmph?

Did something bad happen? Sounds like it.

Am I supposed to ask? Probably not. Let it go... She's a knife-wielding teenager.

But I feel the temptation.

I clear my throat. Then ask—softly:

"Is it... complicated?"

"Nope."

Right back to work. Sharpening her trusty sashimi knife while humming the theme song from *Sazae-san*.

Of course, her presence in Kate wasn't sanctioned by the Governor of Tokyo. She was "unlicensed". Yeah. Nice ring to it.

Kate had to work around her schedule. We called last order early, so her morning commute to school in Kita ward wouldn't be a strain for her. Our lunch menu was limited to dishes that could be served cold or heated up in the micro-wave. But that didn't mean we lowered our standards. Not with her. She kept her eye on the ball. And she really knew her stuff. Me? I was just technically in charge.

Every day, after school, she hit the kitchen. By five-thirty, everything was ready to go. Then, from six, she was a school-girl possessed—by the spirit of the knife.

God. What a sight.

Starting on 20th July—Ocean Day—she worked a full load. No more school. One hundred per cent Knife Girl. Did summer break actually come through for once? Under summer's suspicious auspices, Kate had its second full-time chef.

During Obon, she tells me, "I was really happy to take my brother's spot..." She's wearing goggles and gripping a mini-torch in her left hand. "It got me out of Hatchobori."

She triggers the flame and brings the surface of the crème brûlée to a crisp.

"You mean—there *was* something?"

I ask from the double-pump coffee machine.

"A lot of things..."

"A lot of things?"

No answer.

Well—it came days later. Under her breath: "My dad did a horrible thing..." She was standing by the mixer, fine-tuning a dessert of her own creation, a black sesame *shiruko* we named "Edgar Allan". (By the way, this was not Kate's first homage to the Master of the Macabre. We also had a chocolate cake we called "The Raven".)

Taken aback, I say: "A horrible thing?"

"Yeah... It's kinda hard to explain. I mean, he never hit me or anything. I just..."

"Yeah?"

She shakes her head. "Never mind…"

"No, never never mind," says the eavesdropping Hindu.

"Asshole," she says with a quick back fist.

"You're the one who's hitting people," says the Taoist.

Then she thwacks *him* with the handle of her sashimi knife. Only the Romanian Christian holds his tongue. A wise decision. Well—he barely understands Japanese, so…

The Power of Kate. One big happy family. Long live the Trojan Horse!

Then summer break came to an end. Meaning my teenage chef was back to juggling school and work—not that there was any drop in the quality of her work or whatever. But, wait, there was something I wanted to say about that summer. *It wasn't cursed.* It didn't come to a grinding halt like when I was ten or eleven. It didn't drag on forever like when I was nineteen. And that got me wondering. *Was The Power of Kate working?* It looked like it. I mean, I managed to escape Tokyo's usual havoc, for once. Without even leaving the city.

We made it through the summer. *We* did.

The first-person plural refers to me and my Knife Girl. The tale of my third love stands alone in the annals of my history. This time around, things really begin when the summer ends.

It was towards the end of September—more than two weeks after she went back to school—when she filled me in on the Hatchobori drama. It was a weirdly quiet day at Kate.

One server had food poisoning and called in sick (eel liver was the culprit); another had to go home early (something about "the vault of heaven"?); the last server left right on schedule—without even saying goodbye.

She and I were the only ones around. She was making the next day's lunches, and I was—you know—doing the books.

After her knife-cleaning routine, she started to talk.

I was at the counter, facing her.

"I... um..."

"Huh?"

"..."

The only noise in the room was coming from the ventilator.

"You know, I've been playing with blades ever since I was a kid..."

"Blades?" Meaning *knives*?

"Like this." She lifts up a razor-sharp fish knife, letting it catch the light.

"In my house, they were always around. I guess I liked the way they sparkled. Legendary blades give off a really intense light... and that caught my eye, or—like—maybe hypnotized me. My dad taught me all the basics. He never stopped to think about how I was just a baby. On my third birthday, I pinned down my own eel, slit it open, gutted it, broiled it and made sushi. I had a fish knife that I used for everything until I was like five. Then I branched out into other blades: sashimi, *kamagata*, *mukimono*... I was on TV, on Junior Chef Championship, and came in second. They called me 'Girl Genius'. I was in second grade, maybe third, but I could scale a fish better than any of the middle-school kids."

"Whoa..."

"It was like child's play for me. I've lived with knives my whole life. I've come close to losing a finger so many times I lost track. When everyone else my age was holding a milk bottle, I was gripping my boning knife. This is what I was born to do. That's why my dream was... going into the family business or whatever..."

"Like, take over?"

"Not really. I mean, my brother was around, so I knew I was never going to take my dad's spot. I just thought— you know—I could open a sister shop or something. All I needed was the family name... or, like, part of it. I wanted to make my living with knives, with food. And I was serious about it. I was really really really into traditional Japanese cooking... Or, like, Edo-style with a modern twist. That was my dream."

"Sounds great to me," I say.

"To *you*!" she screams. "I was blind as a Bodhisattva. I totally misinterpreted what my dad was doing. I really thought he cared about me. One day, he looks me right in the eye and says, 'I know what you're thinking—but forget it. This business is no place for girls. Believe me, you'll never make it!' Just thinking about it makes my blood boil. He didn't want me in the family business at all. Everything he taught me was just... supposed to make me a better house-wife! I mean, are you fucking serious!?"

"What the fuck..."

"Right, boss? Maybe he meant well, I dunno, but he swore he'd never let me get behind the counter. I lost my shit. Don't get me wrong. I know where he's coming from, I really do. It's hard for anybody to make it in that world—and the men in this line of work eat women alive... Now more than ever. Before the bubble burst, Hatchobori had it all, tons of places to eat and work—but it's not like that any more. Now it's nothing but parking lots. But where else can you go? Nihonbashi? Ningyocho? My dad knew the odds were against me. So he picked me off. Like in baseball. You know? But, but... Aaugh!"

"It's OK. Let it out."

"Thanks, boss... Yeah, my dad and I collided, we collided head-on. But my brother was there and he stood up for me. He was, like, 'Yeah, living by the knife is tough... but you're no softie. You're tough, you're a diehard.' When my dad heard that, he went apeshit. He beat the crap out of my brother—then he disowned him, which was when my brother started having run-ins with the law."

Now I get it.

"When my brother called and told me he hurt his back, I didn't think twice. Of course I was going to look after him. I owe him big, and I hate being at home and... and... and..."

"And?"

She runs around the counter, right up to me—knife in hand!

"... and I love you!" she says, squeezing me tight.

Huh?

"Boss—you cut right through me."

Say what?

"You believe in me. I mean, I'm your Knife Girl, right? One hundred per cent? It makes me wanna cry. Just me being here could get you in trouble with the law. But you never even flinched..."

She's right about that. I never gave it a thought...

"I can tell you've been fighting too—with everything you've got. You're strong. And you're protecting me—like my own guardian Śakra. You don't even know it, but you saved me. Really. You gave me a chance. To fight against this idiotic world. And I'm not gonna give up. I'm not. You know I'm not."

Knife Girl versus the World. And I thought Kate was *my* fortress.

She had burnt some bridges, too.

I told her everything I wanted from her. Not as my Knife Girl. As my girl.

Love.

She was my third girlfriend. My schoolgirl chef from the east.

It's fall, 2000 A.D. We go out. We go places. With phantom 2,000-yen notes stuffed in our wallets. We start in Koenji. We go to see her brother—my first chef. Then we go exploring. We shop for food at Queen's Isetan, for clothes on Look Street. We buy shirts. A long-sleeve covered in mahjong tiles for me; a short-sleeve with a tarantula print for her. Then we just wander around the area, making fun of all the second-hand stores. Steering clear of Hatchobori, drifting slowly towards the core of Tokyo—Edo? We go east, to eat *monja* in Tsukishima. The way my grandparents see it, she tells me, this place isn't Edo... Because it's reclaimed land or whatever. But the *monja* tastes great, right? We head back. We savour the view from Aioi Bridge at night. Sumida River, the Harumi Canal. We can see Koto ward in the distance. When we enter Chuo ward, we pick up the faint scent of newly printed books.

So many sluices.

So many bridges.

That's what we see. When we go out. When Kate is closed. The rest of the time, we're perfectly happy in our fortress. Kate is our little universe. Our way out of Tokyo, even if we never really leave.

She was the heart of our fortress. The heart of me.

Needless to say, there was no happy ending in the cards. The world would beat me down, like it always does. Beat *us* down? No. Her future was wide open—I was the only one who was going to lose everything.

Mere moments before everything fell apart, I ran into an old friend. I definitely need to mention him here. Because he wrote the chronicle. He was a really good guy, I swear. But his timing was fucking abysmal—like a soothsayer with nothing soothing to say.

It was a December afternoon at Kate. I was sitting at the counter, racking my brains over potential logos for the place. I guess I thought Kate could use a new look—for the new century.

Something like a flag... A declaration of Kate's independence.

From Tokyo.

Then things started getting busy. A ton of orders were coming in and drinks were piling up on the counter. I didn't serve, as a rule, but I did when things got too hectic. So I checked the orders, then took an espresso to a corner table; I didn't get a good look at the customer—his face was hidden behind massive fern fronds. But I could tell that he was about my age.

Him (looking up at me in disbelief): Huh?

Me: You didn't want an espresso?

Him: For real?

Me: Huh?

Him: You—you're... (He says my name. Well, a nickname I had back in high school.)

Now the disbelief is mine. I give him a good look—when it hits me like a piano.

Me: Seriously? Nohara?

Him: In the flesh.

Nohara and I were in the same grade. Remember what I said before? About high school. About being a quiet kid. About *Japanese for idiots*. We had our own words. Words that will live forever—when the chronicle of my life is finally put into writing.

Him: What are you doing here?

Me: I run this place. What are *you* doing here?

Him: You run this place? Wow. You? In business?

It bothers me how he seems sort of impressed.

Him: Great work. I guess I'm here for work, too. To cover the place.

Me: What do you mean?

I didn't keep tabs on old classmates (I was too busy working), so I had no idea what Nohara did for a living. "'The river flows on, but the water is never the same.' We read that in high school. Remember?" he asks. (Yeah, I remember. Opening lines from *The Ten-Foot Hut*. Obviously.) Then he pulls a stack of glossy magazines out of his bag.

Him: I write stuff like this.

His magazines are full of coloured Post-its, marking the pages with his own articles. He's a writer now. Does some freelance editing, too. I take a look at his prose... Surprisingly readable. Nowhere near as devious as it used to be. "The pen is not the man," I guess. Speaking of which...

Me: What the hell is this name? Kaku Nohara?

Him: Me.

Me: I know Nohara. Where did Kaku come from?

Him: It's my pen name. Cool, right? Now my full name means "Heartfield..." *Teeheehee*.

What the hell is he grinning about?

Nothing's changed. Almost like there had been no decade-long blank. If we had a deck of cards, we could have played "Poorest of the Poor"—just the two of us. Like we did in high school. A couple of hours after our chance reunion, we meet up at a local oden place. This time, on purpose. By appointment. When we're done eating, Nohara puts our private patois on hold for a moment—for the sake of business: "If you're OK with it, I'd love to write a longer piece about your place. It'll make a great story."

His face tells me that he means it.

The piece he has in mind, the one he wants me to OK, is tentatively titled: "168 Hours in a Café: Twenty-Four Hours x Seven Days". As Nohara puts it: a photo-essay on everything that goes on inside a popular café. Yeah, right. Kate's no fucking café (not to me), and words like "popular" trip my gag reflex... (But, damn... It's the perfect cover. To help keep my Trojan Horse off the radar. What the hell should I say?) OK, someone just shut me up. I'm way overthinking this.

"Go for it," I say.

I mean, it's Nohara. I've always trusted him. Still do.

Nohara spent about two weeks working on the piece. I spoke, he wrote. I told him pretty much everything. The truth about Kate. About what Kate meant to me. I was totally honest—on the condition that he left those details out of the final product. Now that I think about it, I guess that was the first time I really told anyone about Kate's humble origins.

The story of Kate—transmitted in full. Recorded for posterity. Almost like some sort of sign that all would soon be lost.

Like it had been fated.

Why, God?

Why is the universe teeming with random forces of evil?

It was December—probably late December. I can't remember the date, and I'm sure I don't have to remind you why I forget what I forget. It was a little after ten in the morning, and I was walking down Nakasugi Avenue. Heading for my fortress... Our fortress. But, from a couple of hundred metres away, I could see that something wasn't right. Kate didn't look the same. Is the roof...? From where I stood, the lines looked sort of *wrong*. Kind of like a badly drawn imitation of the real thing.

Then that old whip cracks. Red alert. Alarm bells ringing. *BEEP BEEP BEEP BEEP.*

Not a good sign.

I start running.

Then—the epilogue.

I hurry to unlock the door and witness the carnage inside. *The city stormed my fortress.* The ceiling's punctured in three or four places—holes around fifty centimetres in diameter. *My Trojan Horse has been compromised.* The sun shoots down through the holes, pointing fingers of light at the intruders. That's right. They're still there.

This is the epilogue. Counter in pieces, ferns in smithereens, oven useless on its side. Among all the debris, the chunks of ice that did it.

They were probably three or four massive ice bricks when they hit the roof—before breaking up on impact.

Our territory was ruined.

I stumble over to the biggest block of ice. Glistening in the morning sun. I make a fist and I punch that stupid block. Over and over and over.

And over... and over...

Until my knuckles bleed.

Give me back my horse... You motherfucker...

*

Following a two-month investigation, the Suginami police conclude that a large amount of ice broke loose from the undercarriage of an American fighter jet and fell out of the sky. They might even have an eyewitness. Someone who saw the crash.

So fucking what?

My insurance won't cover this. Looks like the end.

BOAT SEVEN

THIS ISN'T THE FIRST AND YOU KNOW IT'S NOT THE LAST

Mid-April, 2001. About a year and a half ago. I took my third girlfriend (aka "Knife Girl") to the airport. I saw her off—like some kind of guardian. I was twenty-five or twenty-six. Pretty sure we looked nothing like lovers.

Is that because we loved each other too much?

That March, she graduated from the school in Kita ward where she'd spent the last six years. Next stop: the US, the East Coast, where she could fulfil her destiny. Kate—our Asagaya fortress—had been her destiny, but that place was no more. She needed a new place now. She was a knife girl and she needed to fight. I believed that. So I did some digging. Making connections was surprisingly easy. Nohara put me in touch with an editor working on a project called "A Tale of Three Cities: Japanese Taste Around the World". After that, it only took three letters, two international calls and one video (showcasing Knife Girl's literal chops). And the cherry on top: we had the US Ambassador try her cooking and put in a good word, in an unofficial capacity.

I hope you brought your sunglasses. This girl's future was as bright as a 10,000-watt light.

Go West, Knife Girl. You've burnt some bridges—but your blades will get you where you need to go.

She walks through the gate, then looks back. She's sobbing. "Thanks for everything, boss," she shouts. You've got it all wrong. I'm nobody's boss now.

Golden Week is coming at the end of the month—but the airport is unnaturally quiet.

I watch her leave.

I *watched* her leave.

Then I was overcome by an unbearable emptiness.

This is the record of my defeat.

My failed Tokyo Exodus. *It's cold here—too cold.*

Christmas Eve, 2002. Where am I? Ariake Station, on the Yurikamome Line. I walk through the gate and take the long escalator down. Mere metres in front of me: International Exhibition Station on the Rinkai Line. Time to switch trains. But which way? Tennozu Isle or Shin-Kiba? I go—where I'm taken. I don't choose my platform. My platform chooses me. Time moves me.

I trace Tokyo's outline underground.

A voice announces the next station: Shinonome—"dawn".

The train passes through the station, keeps going. Towards the end of the Rinkai Line.

Here it is. Shin-Kiba. Where the Keiyo Line runs above ground and the Yurakucho Line runs underground. They're waiting for me. The wickets call to me, but I don't fall for their trap. I move towards sea level. Listen—I say to myself—you've got your limits. You will die at some point... that's why you can't stop now.

You can't turn your back on the dream.

You can't turn your back on the plan.

You're still alive. Right? Don't give up on getting out—not now.

Then I see it.

The area map. I'm staring right at it. I can't believe my eyes. It's Yume-no-shima. Translation: "Dream Island". A man-made island that dates back to the sixties. A landfill made out of surplus soil.

An island made of trash—for keeping even more trash.

This is what dreams are made of. Yume-no-shima.

Be still, my beating fucking heart.

I walk straight for it.

The place is a park now. It has everything: baseball diamonds, soccer fields, an archery range, a gym, an indoor pool, a bike path. There's even a tropical greenhouse—and eucalyptus everywhere. I follow Meiji Avenue into the park. I head right, over Eucalyptus Bridge. This place has all kinds of palm trees. One kind after another, almost like a family tree of palm trees. There's a footpath near the stadium. I follow it.

Doesn't seem to be anyone around.

I can't see much. There are bushes and trees in my way. But I feel it. *I'm close*. To this place—to this Island of Dreams. I keep walking and come to a clearing...

A crater.

Or is it?

A huge bowl opens up in front of me. It looks just like a crater made by a meteorite. The coliseum—the pride of the park. But there's no one here. Not today, not now. I see no actors onstage at the bottom of the bowl. No gladiators trying to dismember one another. No Ancient Roman orators come back to life. The absence thrills me to no end.

I feel it. *It's here.*

But what is?

I don't know. Not yet.

The bowl doesn't have seats. Just stone steps that double as seats. I sit down—on the third or fourth step. Some pigeons on the next block take off when I crash the party. I wrap my arms around my knees. I can feel myself becoming part of the stone (hard, cold, artificial). Then I go to sleep. I could almost hear the thud. As I break through.

Through the wall dividing reality and dreams.

Thud.

I'm lying down this time. On that single bed. The bed in that "room". I was asleep—but I'm up now. I'm holding something. Against my chest. The CD. I was sleeping with Sonny Rollins in my arms. It had to be the CD. Because it's too important to let go.

Track eleven tells me everything I need to know. The truth. This is no hotel. This is no "room".

On a Slow Boat to China.

That explains the vibrations—the buzz of the bed. But it isn't the bed. It's everything. The whole... vessel.

I'm on a slow boat.

I get out of bed. I know what I'm looking for. Where is it? I take half a step towards the desk. Brush away the heaps of dust. *It kind of looks like snow.* Something's speeding up now. Getting faster. Time? I start digging. It has to be here somewhere. That slip of paper.

Found it. My ticket to ride.

The words are a blur. Can't make them out.

Time is moving dangerously fast now.

Where am I going? *Where's this slow boat taking me?* Hope... I still have hope. That I'm getting out of here. But I have no idea where I am—no idea where I'm going—and isn't that the same as having no way out? The floor rumbles, speaks to me: *You're not going anywhere.* The room has shape now. The shape of a cabin. Better hurry.

The rumbling doesn't stop. It's hypnotizing. *This isn't the first and you know it's not the last. There's nothing you can do, nowhere you can go.*

Then I hear another voice. *You're wrong,* she says.

Softly.

The window's boarded up. It won't let the outside in. The door is no good. The knob is dead. Got to get to the bottom of this. Or do you wanna be a fossil? You wanna turn to dust—trapped in this cabin? No fucking way.

I sail with my mind.

Like riding a dragon. Like in that movie, when the hero flies to the end of the world. *To keep the world from ending.* The scene plays back in my head.

Back to the bathroom. I step inside. Look at the mirror. It's still cloudy. I wipe it clean with the bottom of my fist to find myself looking back at me. Is that really me? A question like the last judgement. Yes, I answer.

Yes. This is my life.
And I won't run.
From my chronicle of failures.

In that moment, I slip through the wall—through the mirror.
Into the real "dream".

And I don't wake up.

CHRONICLE

−2000−

We read the human genome. Mar. 31: Mt. Usu in Hokkaido erupted—*after* the region had been evacuated. It was the first time volcanic activity had been predicted beforehand. The leaders of North and South Korea had their first tête-à-tête in fifty-five years. Aug. 12: an atomic submarine sank in the Barents. The entire crew—118 souls—perished. Milošević's dictatorship fell. Naoko Takahashi won gold in Sydney. The 20th century came to an end.

STARBUCKS OVERKILL
By Kaku Nohara

Right on time. There's a knock at the door. But you can't come in if you don't know the password. Millimetres behind the door, I whisper the prompt: "Chiang".

From the other side of the door: "Kai-shek".

Permission granted. I unlock the triple-bolt and let my comrade in. It's Fumio Narazaki.

"Pretty little mess you got here. How about cleaning up every year or so?"

"I clean all the time—like, every other month."

"And another thing," Fumio Narazaki says, "do we need really need a password? It's not like we're samurai

from the Edo period or something... Hey, where is everybody?" He looks around the room.

"Hate to break it to you..." I make a sour face. "It's just us. The others are busy with their real jobs..."

"Seriously? It's just us?"

"Sucks lemons, I know."

"Shit," Fumio Narazaki says, "my boss asked me to stay late, too. But I told him to take his overtime and stuff it. I came because you said this was the 'case to end all cases'."

"Oh, it is. It's huge."

"How huge?"

I point him towards the open notebook in the middle of the war zone that I call my room. Narazaki and I lean in—our heads almost hit—and we re-enter The Incidents of Coincidence. Just like we have since we were kids.

Case one: Private Residence. Arakicho, Yotsuya. An office worker on the way home from a ramen joint broke into her ex-lover's apartment and killed him. The victim's wife also sustained serious injuries. The suspect filled their mouths with large quantities of dried seaweed. Her confession: "He was never going to leave her... so I had to do something to shut his lying mouth for good."

Case two: An office complex in Ryogoku's third district. A taxi driver deep in debt killed three loan sharks. His weapon: a couple of chanko pots.

Case three: Numabukuro. On Asahi Avenue. A boy (sixteen years old) stabbed a housewife with a thirty-centimetre hunting blade purchased on the Internet.

Over ten hours later, authorities learn that the victim was the suspect's biological mother.

"Same as ever—the world's totally unhinged..." Fumio Narazaki sighs. "I know snowballing interest can be a real nightmare, but to end the lives of a few loan sharks with ceramic pots..."

"There's more, though. Check this out..."

I show him photos from the three crime scenes. I've circled items in red.

"Something hidden?"

"What do you think?"

"..."

"See that Starbucks cup on the ground? Caramel macchiato, according to the investigation. That's the key to this bloody tale of ramen and revenge. The cup was the killer's—she was sipping that macchiato moments before committing murder. It's a fact. A fact that the authorities and the media have completely neglected."

"Interesting."

"Unusual, right?"

"Ramen and Starbucks? Highly unusual."

"Next scene. Ryogoku. Shards everywhere, and... here."

Fumio Narazaki eyeballs the photograph for a few seconds.

"A tall, right?"

"Precisely. Café latte."

"And it was the driver's drink?"

"These sharks don't drink coffee. It's been corroborated."

"All right. What about Numabukuro? Got it... Next to the pool of blood. Let me guess. Café mocha?"

"Bingo."

"Tall again, I see."

Fumio Narazaki snarls.

Now for the hard question. What led these three Starbucks drinkers to commit murder? What's the connection? First hypothesis: "Some kind of complex?" Maybe, maybe not. In no time, our conversation turns away from the three crime scenes. Back to the café that links them all.

"OK, OK—what about Starbucks?" I ask. "Guilty?"

"Wait, what's the charge?"

"Crimes against Tokyo, I guess."

"Not guilty. Got to say, I think Bucks has done more good than evil..."

"Seriously?"

"Beats McDonald's—they only want families, family money. At least Starbucks is open to all types. People of all creeds and classes..."

"Starbucks was sort of exclusive... at least at first..."

"But it's different now. Men and women, all ages, go to Starbucks—and they go for the coffee. It's not like other chains, like Doutor, where people go to smoke. I dunno. My verdict: Starbucks has raised Tokyo's quality of life."

"I can get behind that."

"Of course you can. It's almost like, like Starbucks set us free."

"Shit... That's it."

"What's what?"

"Starbucks set us free..."

"Wait, from what?"

"From life's unwritten rules. Like, suck it up, deal with it. All that. Now you can go to Bucks... Enjoy a caramel macchiato..."

"Yeah yeah yeah. The killers smelt the coffee—and woke up. Like, 'I should end that fucking liar's life. Fuck it, his wife had it coming, too...'"

"I guess that's one kind of enlightenment..."

We sit there in silence for a minute.

"Pretty sure we cracked it."

"Cool."

Case closed. Time to celebrate. We open a bottle of sparkling wine and pour it into the Starbucks cups I'd prepared as evidence. We put the lids on and watch the bubbles ooze through the slits. Then we raise our grandes and take a swig.

Pop, pop, pop. Goodbye, my year 2000.

BOAT EIGHT
AND KEEP YOUR HEAD UP

Hello.

I imagine this letter comes as a surprise. We've never met, but please read this to the end. I'll get right to it. You once knew someone very close to me.

My sister.

My older sister. Technically, we're half-sisters. We have different fathers. But that has nothing to do with what I want to tell you.

I'm a lot younger than my sister. I'm only nineteen. I started taking care of her as soon as I finished high school. Like a nurse. It was a long battle. Over two years. But it's over now. In the spring, I'll start college somewhere. The only reason I can even think about going to school is because she's gone.

She passed away in the fall.

What she had wasn't the sort of thing that gets better. But the hardest part for me (and the most painful part for her) wasn't the hopelessness, not really. It was the contradiction—the fact that she had to keep getting treatment even though things were never going to turn around. I don't know. Maybe "contradiction" isn't the right word. Everyone knew how it was going to end. But she still spent the last two years of her life in pyjamas and slippers...

I loved my sister. That's why I didn't mind looking after her. She told me all sorts of stories. She let me into her life. It was almost like being in love. How can I put this? Nursing someone means being their shadow. Her routine became mine. My own life was a total blank, and it was filled with my sister's memories. Something like that. Like I became the book of her life.

And in that book you *play a major role.*

I know it's hard to believe, but I'm serious. You may not even remember her. You've probably forgotten her name, her face—everything. You only had a month together, and it was back in grade school.

In the mountains.

"But," she told me, "that's where I was saved."

You *saved her.*

She told me that many times. In her own words: "He was the one who taught me to talk with the world. To speak so that others could understand. Until the summer of sixth grade, I was only sleeping—living in a dream world. Then he came along and woke me up."

She called you her summer-school sweetheart.

After that summer she had a normal life. She got married— maybe a little earlier than most people get married these days. She was in her early twenties. A couple of years later, she found out that she was sick.

But fate's not bad or good. A few months after she started going to the hospital, we were in the waiting room, flipping through magazines. That's when we saw this article—"The Café Vanishes"—which was about this place you used to run. It had your name in it, and a small photo of you. (I have to say, it didn't look like you wanted to have your photo taken.)

My sister knew it was you, right away.

I'm glad I found a way to reach you. Now that I have, I need to say something from my sister:

"Thank you."

And, from me, too. Thank you. For everything you did to make my sister thankful. I learnt a lot from her—about courage, about love. My sister lives on, inside of me. Can I tell you the last thing she said to me?

"Stand tall—and keep your head up."

I'm enclosing something for you—from her and me. I know it's strange, since we've never even met. I just wanted you to have it. My sister really loved this CD. She was always listening to it—even at the hospital, on headphones. Her favourite was track eleven. It's a standard number called "On a Slow Boat to China".

I don't know why I'm telling you this, but her husband was Chinese. He runs a small import business in Yokohama.

That's probably what kept pulling her back to that track. She was always listening to it.

Up to the end.

Goodbye. I hope this letter reaches you.

LAST BOAT
TO CHINA

I tried using a map, but no luck. The topography was unclear. If I'm reading the compass right, I'm somewhere west of the Amami Islands. But no ocean means no islands...

The East China Sea is nothing but desert. But I keep my head.

I learn what I can from the campers—where I can get my hands on potable water, cans of food, etc. Bartering is dangerous business, but sustenance is necessary. It just drives home the point—*you do what you can to stay alive.*

Sometimes surviving means flirting with death.

I check my water supply, drink the bare minimum. In these parts, they sell water in 1.5-litre bottles with Diet Pepsi labels on them.

The sun is my greatest enemy—I try to stay out of its way. And there are nomadic tribes all around (some are just bands of savage children), so I can't afford to drop my guard. Sometimes I stumble upon the aftermath of their marauding deeds. I see paw prints. Some gangs must be running attack hounds.

When I regained consciousness, I spent two full days walking. No leads on any waterways. Then, this morning, I looked up at the blue blue sky—there were birds flying right over me.

*

I heard a steam whistle. A weird whistle—kind of like a tenor sax.

Then, way off in the distance, I saw the shape of a ship.

No, I tell myself, it isn't that far. Do the math. It's headed this way, right? Got to get a read on the sail. Got to get ahead of the ship. Got to start footing it.

The soles of my feet were burning up, but I kept going.

After three hours, I came to a thin strip of water. Just wide enough for a single cargo ship. In fact, one was coming this way.

A sailor asks from the deck: "Need a lift?"

I don't nod.

"No?" he asks.

"Where you going?"

"What, this freighter?"

"Yeah."

"To China," he says.

I inform the sailor of my desire to board.

"OK, one ticket. To China."

WRITING ABOUT WHAT I'M WRITING ABOUT

This book demands explanation. You open it up to find the title on the title page. Fair enough. But then there's a sub-title under it. A strange subtitle—right? You keep going, but the Contents page is no less strange. Some readers might wonder: "Where have I seen these words before? They look kind of familiar."

These chapter titles are borrowed. Phrases lifted from the work of another writer.

I've sampled them.

Maybe that sounds a little too musical. But I've never been the sort of writer who lives in an entirely literary world. Pop culture is the air I breathe. I know how it feels to put a record on a turntable, to flip it over and play the other side. And I know how it feels to grip a gamepad or dip my hand into a bag of chips while watching a movie. But *music* has probably given me the most, and it just keeps giving me more.

Maybe the best gift of all: music has shown me how to *survive*.

Music comes in many forms. Radio, tape, CD. But the song has a way of moving on its own—from generation to generation. Take the cover song. Singing the hits of the past today. With nothing but the deepest respect for those who came before.

Like with the early Beatles or the Stones. The way they did it.

Now.

There's no reason you can't do the same thing with stories. To take your love for the original and situate it in the present. Back to this book. To the subtitle: *A Slow Boat to China RMX*. A nod to Haruki Murakami's unforgettable short story—"A Slow Boat to China". The story where my story begins.

For me, Murakami is at the centre of it all—the roots of my soul.

RMX stands for "remix". Remixes, covers... It's easy to get them mixed up. But "misreading" is a big part of what this book is about, so I hope you'll forgive me. Whenever I think about remixing, I think about this one story I know. It has to do with a well-known remixer, whose name I forget. When an artist comes to him for a track, he doesn't run to the studio. He puts the song on repeat and goes to bed. He lets it play all night. Then, when he wakes up in the morning, he knows exactly what to do.

That's what I'm talking about when I talk about remixing.

Unconsciousness. Dreams. And love that has no value other than purity.

This book is dedicated to Tokyo, 2002—and all the years that went into making it.

And to the roots of my soul. Hope he doesn't mind.

Pushkin Press

Pushkin Press was founded in 1997, and publishes novels, essays, memoirs, children's books—everything from timeless classics to the urgent and contemporary.

Our books represent exciting, high-quality writing from around the world: we publish some of the twentieth century's most widely acclaimed, brilliant authors such as Stefan Zweig, Marcel Aymé, Teffi, Antal Szerb, Gaito Gazdanov and Yasushi Inoue, as well as compelling and award-winning contemporary writers, including Andrés Neuman, Edith Pearlman, Eka Kurniawan and Ayelet Gundar-Goshen.

Pushkin Press publishes the world's best stories, to be read and read again. Here are just some of the titles from our long and varied list. To discover more, visit www.pushkinpress.com.

═══

THE SPECTRE OF ALEXANDER WOLF
GAITO GAZDANOV
'A mesmerising work of literature' Antony Beevor

SUMMER BEFORE THE DARK
VOLKER WEIDERMANN
'For such a slim book to convey with such poignancy the extinction of a generation of "Great Europeans" is a triumph' *Sunday Telegraph*

MESSAGES FROM A LOST WORLD
STEFAN ZWEIG
'At a time of monetary crisis and political disorder... Zweig's celebration of the brotherhood of peoples reminds us that there is another way' *The Nation*

BINOCULAR VISION
EDITH PEARLMAN
'A genius of the short story' Mark Lawson, *Guardian*

IN THE BEGINNING WAS THE SEA
TOMÁS GONZÁLEZ

'Smoothly intriguing narrative, with its touches of sinister, Patricia Highsmith-like menace' *Irish Times*

BEWARE OF PITY
STEFAN ZWEIG

'Zweig's fictional masterpiece' *Guardian*

THE ENCOUNTER
PETRU POPESCU

'A book that suggests new ways of looking at the world and our place within it' *Sunday Telegraph*

WAKE UP, SIR!
JONATHAN AMES

'The novel is extremely funny but it is also sad and poignant, and almost incredibly clever' *Guardian*

THE WORLD OF YESTERDAY
STEFAN ZWEIG

'*The World of Yesterday* is one of the greatest memoirs of the twentieth century, as perfect in its evocation of the world Zweig loved, as it is in its portrayal of how that world was destroyed' David Hare

WAKING LIONS
AYELET GUNDAR-GOSHEN

'A literary thriller that is used as a vehicle to explore big moral issues. I loved everything about it' *Daily Mail*

BONITA AVENUE
PETER BUWALDA

'One wild ride: a swirling helix of a family saga… a new writer as toe-curling as early Roth, as roomy as Franzen and as caustic as Houellebecq' *Sunday Telegraph*

JOURNEY BY MOONLIGHT
ANTAL SZERB

'Just divine… makes you imagine the author has had private access to your own soul' Nicholas Lezard, *Guardian*